I0658465

October 32

Larry Rodness

DEER HAWK
PUBLICATIONS

OCTOBER 32 is published by:
Deer Hawk Publishing, an imprint of
Deer Hawk Enterprises
www.deerhawkpublications.com

Copyright © 2015 by Larry Rodness

All rights reserved. Without limiting copyrights listed above,
no part of this publication may be reproduced, stored in a
retrieval system or transmitted in any form or by any means:
electronic, mechanical, photocopying, recording or otherwise
without prior written permission of the copyright owner and/or
the publisher, except for excerpts quoted in the context of
reviews.

This is a work of fiction. Names, characters, places, brands,
media and incidents portrayed in this book are either the
product of the author's imagination or are used fictitiously.

Cover design by:
Erin Rodness

Layout by:
Aurelia Sands

Printed in the United States of America

Acknowledgement: to my writing colleagues Reva, Diane, Herb and Marsha for their abundant criticism and support.

To my wife, Jodi, and all my children including Sophie
for their patience and love.

CHAPTER 1

I love my job. I love my life. I love trundling down the highway with the morning sun riding shotgun on my shoulder as I head to my next assignment. This week, I've been sent to a picturesque little town that sits on the edge of the Grand River. I'm rarely in the big cities anymore, which, for me, is one of the great joys in life. I'm free of the heavy traffic, the suicide bike messengers, and the dumb-ass pedestrians who walk blindly across the streets with their heads buried in their smart phones. All I have to contend with these days is the odd squirrel challenging me to a game of chicken as he makes a mad dash across the road. Every time I face off with one of these fearless little guys, I wonder what he's thinking, *This is my turf. Stay off it,* or, *I'm gonna beat this guy if it kills me*, or, *Is it my time to die?* When he makes his decision to venture out on the road, I wonder whether he has a sense that he's tempting fate. Do I?

I roll down my window to get a whiff of the fresh manure that wafts lazily in the autumn air. It's an odor I'd take over carbon monoxide fumes or the manufactured smell of air conditioning any day. The breeze on my face is surprisingly mild for an October morning. God bless Indian summers, global warming, or El Nino—whatever has taken hold of the countryside. My drive takes me blissfully along this narrow ribbon of asphalt past fields of ripe pumpkins and corn where farm hands have been loading heavy bushels of produce onto wagons since dawn. I nod and smile neighborly when I pass as if these people were personal friends or prospective clients. Who knows, they may very well be. My job takes me to places like Wellington County every week to discuss how to protect families when death takes a loved one. I say "when," not "if," because it's inevitable—even though many refuse to face it. Death and taxes, the only certainties in life, right? I'm here to help the farmers, the pensioners, and the retirees face that fact and to provide them with the peace of mind they've either put off or ignored all their lives. Which brings me back to my little friend, the squirrel, and his Zen-like approach to mortality–a quality that many of my clients could benefit from.

There's the sign I'm looking for on my right, "WELCOME TO ELORA." I glance down at my appointment book buried under half-eaten squares of toast. My first meeting of the morning is scheduled for 10:30, which means I've arrived an hour early. I like to book seven appointments a day, but Elora takes its Halloween seriously and I could only get five. No matter, "I'll be here all week," as they say.

A flock of crows perched on an overhead telephone wire watches my approach. Odd, how their heads lift as one when they see me and then they fly toward town. I wonder, *are they trumpeting my arrival, or warning the town?* I hang a right off the highway onto a short, steel-girded bridge that spans the Grand River. The waters below flow directly toward the falls that spill into the spectacular Elora Gorge, one of the natural wonders of the region. The bridge delivers me directly onto Metcalfe Street, the main drag of this town. It's early, but the park on the corner is already crowded

2

with locals and tourists meandering through stalls filled with giant pumpkins, antiques, and baked goods. Over the years, this fall event has morphed from a modest harvest festival into a first-class Halloween scare-fair and one of the biggest draws in the county.

Even the business section has been transformed for the holiday. Giant gargoyles, spiders, and demons seem to crawl in and out of buildings. The villagers spend weeks creating them out of papier-mâché and chicken wire, and they are so massive that it actually looks like the town has been overrun by monsters. It's certainly been overrun by cars. There isn't a single parking space available, and it's only after I pass through the commercial area that I find a spot on a side street near a church. Atop its tall, green steeple is the flock of crows that flew in ahead of me. At least it looks like the same flock.

I climb out of my car and straighten my crisp, white shirt and tie. There's also a sports jacket I keep in the back to suit the weather or the type of client I'm meeting. After years on the road, I've learned to be prepared for anything. I give myself a good stretch after the hour-and-a-half drive. I used to be five-foot-nine but in my late-fifties, I think I've reached that point where I'm actually shrinking. I check myself out in the reflection of the passenger window. My hair is thinning and my gut is expanding. If I were honest with myself, I'd admit that my best years are behind me. But I'm not that honest. I've been thinking about hair plugs and lipo, but the truth is, I can't be bothered. I'd have to take too much time off work, and as I said, I love my work.

With a few minutes to spare, I saunter back past the curio shops and restaurants to the park, one of the first things you see when you traverse the bridge. The town has gone to great lengths to make it visually impressive including the bright red benches that surround the lush, green lawn. Little gardens dot the hilly landscape. But the focal point of the park is an impressive statue entitled, "The Tall Man" for obvious reasons. By way of further explanation, there's a plaque at its base that reads, "It's a question of who's in charge." Today, the answer would be the Fall Halloween Festival. It's a joyous event celebrated with costumes and music and the sweet smell of baked goods designed to super-charge the youngsters and play havoc with insulin levels of the elderly. Everyone here is cordial to each other. Even the Amish move comfortably through the crowds.

The only exception is a woman standing on the sidewalk. I notice her because everyone in the vicinity tries to avoid her. It's not that she's ugly or deformed. She's quite attractive, somewhere in her thirties, with shoulder-length, ginger colored hair and a pleasant, outdoorsy look. She's dressed in a billowy blouse and long skirt with a silk kerchief draped around her shoulders like some escaped hippie from the sixties. It's not that I'm critical or judgmental, but I've trained myself to notice details like these because they can make a difference between a sale and a snub. She's studying a playbill pasted on the window of a florist shop that reads, "The Elora Players Present *Brigadoon*," and I chuckle.

"Something funny?" she asks.

"No. I mean, *Brigadoon*. It's kind of an old

musical, isn't it? Not like *Wicked* or *Chicago* or something more contemporary."

"You know the story of *Brigadoon*, Mister…?" she asks.

"…Malefant. Alexander Malefant. I'm not a hundred percent sure, but I think it's set in the Scottish Highlands. It's about a village that wakes up once every 100 years?"

"The inhabitants are forbidden to leave," she adds, "for fear their home will vanish forever."

"Right. Reminds me of that other place—Shangri-La, hidden away in the Himalayan Mountains. I think in that story the people never grow old."

"Ah, but there's a difference. If the villagers leave Brigadoon, the town will vanish forever. If the inhabitants of Shangri-La leave, they will age instantly."

"And what happens here?" I ask as a joke.

"What do you mean?"

"Nothing. I'm just…" Seems like I've put my foot in my mouth a second time.

"You know the common element in the two myths?" asks the woman. "The stranger who upsets the status quo and changes the lives of everyone forever."

"Well, I hope not to disrupt things too much while I'm here," I answer, trying to end on a light note.

"I will hold you to that," she says with a wry smile.

I smile back and turn away, happy to have extricated myself from the awkward conversation; but not quite before things take a curious turn.

"Are you a witch?" asks a little boy. He's

about seven or eight years old, with a dead serious look on his face. Down the block, I notice a group of his buddies anxiously awaiting the woman's response.

"Did your friends dare you to ask me that?" she responds.

The little boy nods, his wary eyes locked onto hers as if with a twitch of her nose she'll turn him into a donkey or a pig.

"You're very brave," says the woman with a warm smile.

"Bruce!"

That nervous call comes from another woman across the street. Must be the boy's mother. I see her waiting in line with her husband and pre-teen daughter for their turn at the apple-bobbing contest. The tall brunette in the tight-fitting green sweater is attractive by rural standards. Again, I'm not judging, but through my travels, I've noticed that a good many men and women in the countryside grow stout from the healthy appetite needed to sustain the hard work that the land demands of them. Not this one though, she could've stepped right off a New York runway. Little Bruce runs across the street to join his yummy mommy while his friends taunt him with catcalls of "chicken" and "pussy." The lady they call a witch walks away, our conversation ended. The funny thing is, she's not wearing a costume or anything remotely witchy-like, so what prompted the boy?

"Everybody say 'pepon'!"

"Pepon!" replies a chorus of voices.

A few feet away, a blonde, middle-aged woman leads an informal talk to a handful of tourists around a large cart with a variety of pumpkins. My interest shifts because her voice is so commanding. But it's worth a listen. Any information or common ground I can use to break the ice with my clients will come in handy later, especially when the subject is death.

"Very good," the tour guide continues. "That's the correct name for the pumpkin, which originally hails from South America. The pepon, or large melon, comes in many varieties including the Small Sugar, the Baby Boo, the Spirit, the Aspen, and the ever-popular Autumn Gold. Some can grow to over 1,000 pounds."

"What's with this damn heat?" remarks a portly gentleman strolling past me with a woman who could only be his wife. As the man tugs uncomfortably at his starched collar, the embarrassed tour guide tries to cover the remark by inviting him into the conversation.

"What a nice surprise! Ladies and gentlemen, Mayor Percy Novak and his lovely wife, Mary."

Caught off guard, the mayor nods and makes his way over.

"Thank you, Betty," he says. "Hope you're all enjoying this beautiful weather we've ordered special for you today, ha-ha. As you know, folks, Elora has been the pumpkin capital of this region for the past fifty years."

The mayor proudly points to the banner that stretches across the lawn, "WELLINGTON COUNTY FALL FESTIVAL & SCARE FAIR." Before he can continue, Betty jumps in.

"...ever since we took the trophy from Fergus, back in '64."

She proudly redirects the crowd's attention

to a large trophy standing on the podium. Not to be upstaged, the mayor points to the tables laden with delicious baked goods, and spreads his meaty arms as if he's offering a benediction, "And we have won every year since."

Someone shouts out, "Sounds like the fix is in."

The good-natured jab takes Betty by surprise, but the mayor responds without missing a beat.

"Couldn't ever happen, friend. Know why? Because before the contest begins, every one of those baked goods are labeled underneath their tins so the judges have no idea what belongs to who. Learned that lesson long time ago. Trust me, folks, everything is on the up and up in Elora and has been for the past fifty years."

I'm hearing a big emphasis on the past fifty years, which begs the question, *What happened before that?*

"So, Mayor, what's your secret?" asks an inquisitive bystander. "How do you keep coming up with these award-winning pies year after year?"

Betty leaps up onto the podium next to the trophy and proclaims, "All the ladies of this town use the same magical ingredient in their cooking: love."

"Yeah, they put an extra dollop in every cow pie," shouts some comedian.

A solemn, gravel-voice cuts through the laughter, "The dirt." The voice belongs to an elderly black fellow dressed in a postman's uniform whom the regulars around here call Titus. "What we put in the dirt pays us back in spades."

Having succeeded in casting a pall over the

festivities, the cranky old coot shuffles across the street to the steps of the church where he joins half a dozen elderly citizens.

Perturbed at losing her audience, Betty tries to get the crowd back. "Now let me introduce you to the pepon's cousin, the squash."

She revs up her dissertation while the mayor glad-hands as many people as he can before he and his wife continue their tour. Every town has its own unique culture, eccentricities, and secrets. I never presume that because I come from the big city, I'm any smarter than anyone else, but sometimes you just have to laugh.

"Bruce? Stop goofing around. Bruce? Somebody help!"

The little boy who was waiting in line with his family has his head submerged in the apple barrel, struggling to get out. If I didn't know better, I'd say he's playing a Halloween prank on his parents, but the distressed looks on their faces tell me otherwise. It almost looks as if something inside is holding him under. Everyone in the vicinity stops what they're doing. Worry and concern are written all over their faces, yet no one does anything. Then, out of the corner of my eye, I see that strange lady race across the lawn, push through the dumb-struck spectators, and knock over the barrel with her shoulder. The water spills out, releasing Bruce and drenching his mother who, in a fit of anger, lashes out at her son's rescuer.

"Missy! You stupid fool!"

The boy is free, but the emergency isn't over. Bruce lays on the grass, limp and unresponsive. His sister continues to scream for help until a police officer makes his way through the crowd. With practiced hands, he turns the boy over and checks for a pulse. Then he sweeps the boy's mouth for any obstructions and finding none, begins performing quick compressions on his chest. After several attempts, the boy finally wretches up a mouth full of water which he then spews onto his mother's shoes, drenching her a second time. If the moment wasn't so unsettling, it would be comical.

"That's it, cough it up, Son," says the officer.

Everyone's eyes are on the boy except the woman they call Missy, who seems preoccupied with the barrel. I follow her gaze and see something slither out; not animal, not mineral, but something jelly-like, almost transparent. Whatever it is seeps into the lawn and disappears. Missy looks up to see if anyone else saw it. I avoid her gaze, unwilling to get pulled into the drama. I'm just a businessman here to do a job. Meanwhile, shouts of thanks are offered to the officer.

"Let's give the boy some room," he says.

After the constable assures everyone that young Bruce is all right, the onlookers step back and I get a better look at him. He's a well-built guy in his thirties, slightly taller than me, with short brown hair, and one of the few around here who has managed to keep trim. His name badge reads, "Clarke." Constable Clarke has a natural air of authority about him, and when he speaks, people listen. "Everybody, the boy is fine. You can all go back now, enjoy your festival." As spectators disperse, the boy's parents swoop in.

"Bruce, are you all right, sweetie? You scared the hell out of us."

A beat later, the mayor barges into the

circle, sounding more bombastic than ever, "Rob, Amanda, I saw everything. What happened?"

"Dunno exactly, Percy," replies Rob. "One minute, Bruce is bobbing for apples, the next minute, he's fightin' for his life."

Amanda takes off her son's shirt and wrings the excess water out of it. Rob ruffles his boy's hair as if to play down the gravity of the situation, while his sister, Erin, gives her brother a warm hug. Then little Bruce speaks for the first time, "Cut it out. I'm all right. I'm okay."

"Can you tell me what happened, Bruce?" asks the constable.

"I dunno. Somethin' grabbed me, like, pulled me under."

Officer Clarke examines the overturned barrel inside and out, but by the look on his face, it's clear he finds nothing suspicious.

"Thanks again, Hubble," says the grateful Amanda.

"She's the one who saved me," corrects Bruce who points to Missy.

Amanda offers Missy a half-hearted thanks. Last, but not least, Betty the tour guide, makes her entrance like a soap opera diva.

"Oh My God, Brucey darling, are you all right?"

"Of course he is, Betty, as you can plainly see," remarks Amanda.

"Well excuse me for being concerned!"

Offended, Betty leaves as quickly as she came. There's obviously a history between these two. The mayor gives young Bruce a pat on the back as if *he* was instrumental in saving him and owes him a vote when he comes of age. With the excitement over, everyone returns to the festivities. I glance at Missy and smile. Contrary to her remark earlier, the new stranger in town has not been the cause of this or any disruption. I return to my car to get my materials. I've got a presentation to make.

CHAPTER 2

"Hi Betty, I'm Alexander Malefant from Hale Insurance."

Betty, the pepon maven, turns out to be my first appointment of the day.

"Love your garden."

When I started in sales, I picked up some CDs by a few noted marketing gurus. There was nothing specific to the insurance industry per se, but the skills were pretty well adaptable to any sales-driven business. The first thing I learned was to be me, not a version of what I thought would appeal to someone else. The second thing was to open every conversation with a compliment. I never lie or try to be disingenuous, but I have anywhere from sixty to ninety minutes to explain the plan and gain the trust of my client. They have to feel comfortable enough with me so that by the end of the presentation, they're prepared to sign a policy because I may not be back for another year. Therefore, it's important to start the relationship off on the best possible note. The compliment may be over something as innocuous as flowers in a garden, or family pictures, or how clean the house appears. Everybody has something they're proud of. I once complimented a man on his sword collection, and another on how neatly he had arranged his arrest record in his scrapbook—before he turned to Jesus, of course.

"Why thank you, Mister Malefant," Betty replies as she shows me into her living room.

"You have quite the flair for color and design." Again I'm not lying. The place is awash in pastel-colored couches, throw pillows, and angular coffee tables. If I had to name the style, I'd call it "Jetson-chic."

"Is there a table we can sit at, Betty, so I can show you everything you need to see?"

I always avoid sitting in the living room, especially if there's a TV on. This is not where business is done.

"Well, there's the kitchen," she says, "It's a little crowded but…"

"Perfect." No TV, no radio, no distractions.

Betty leads me down the hall to her kitchen while I keep my eye out for anything that might give me a clue as to her family makeup or marital status. I see portraits of her and a boy at various stages of growth, but no father figure. Nor are there any references to organizations the man of the house might have on display–Lions Club plaques, team pictures, mounted deer heads. I'm thinking she's either divorced or widowed. When we arrive in the kitchen, the table is covered with a sweater, rolls of Lifesaver candies, and a sewing kit.

"Is this your Halloween costume?"

"A little trick, a little treat, you might say," she says with a sly grin.

"I see your creativity extends to more than…"

"I have a lot planned for this evening, Mister Malefant, so I hope this won't take too long."

"Of course not, and call me Alexander."

Betty sweeps the paraphernalia into her lap and begins to sew the candies onto the sweater while I open my binder and show her the letter we sent her.

"You filled out the bottom of this letter and returned it to us asking for more information about life insurance. Do you recall?"

"Yes, yes I do."

"What do you do, Betty, if I may ask—besides of course, being the town authority on the pepon?"

I have just made her aware that I caught her act in the park and she smiles. That little side-trip to the festival just paid off. Betty relaxes and fills me in on her two part-time jobs, which don't amount to very much. Most of her money comes from her husband, who is conspicuously absent.

"Of course, I don't want my Zack to have to pay any outstanding bills after I'm gone. There's still a mortgage on the house and it's bad enough his father ran off with that little whore, leaving us both with..."

And there it is—a single parent solely responsible for her son, an absent father who has abandoned one family to start another. As if on cue, I hear the sound of a young bull elephant charging down the stairs. A second later a tall, gangly teenager pokes his head around the corner and gives me the once-over. The kid has rugged, good-looking features that could have been carved from a block of wood...and looks as intelligent. But it's those hooded, hazel eyes that speak to me the most—a mixture of indifference, boredom, and deviltry that teenage boys often have.

"Zack, come say hi to..."

Having already concluded there's nothing I have that could benefit him, Zack continues out the door. If this is Betty's singular reason for living, that's fine with me.

"Looks like a bright, young fellow," I comment. "And that's why we're here today,

Betty—to make sure he's not left with an expensive problem. Here's how we're going to do it."

Mortality is a fickle beast. When you're young, it's a winged stallion, all tricked out in silver spurs and a brocade saddle, riding you off into fame and fortune. When you approach middle age, it morphs into a broken-down swayback, carrying you inexorably toward a big, motherfucking precipice from which there is no return. That precipice may still be far off on the horizon, but you're acutely aware that the distance is dwindling, especially when Uncle Jim dies suddenly of a heart attack, and you see the misery Aunt Joan has gone through. The last thing you want is for your family to be as unprepared as she was. So, based on the age and income of my client, I'll suggest term or whole life insurance, or a combination thereof. It all depends on what their objectives are, and that's not always easy to get those out of the client. But, even after I've laid out everything in front of them—the problems and solutions—some will still resist making the commitment. When it comes to putting pen to paper, you often get that deer-in-the-headlight stare and that "I'll have to think about it," response. It's almost as if by signing the insurance policy, they think they're signing their own death certificates. With a little reassurance that we're here to solve a problem, not create one, the only question is how much they can afford. If they're in complete denial, they'll just show me the door as if I'm the Grim Reaper himself.

When I finally get down to dollars and cents with Betty, she puts down her sweater, which now has about two dozen candies sewn onto it in no particular order or design. I point to the figures I've worked out, and she points to the financial plan that works best for her. That's when a chorus of children's voices comes screaming past her front door like a pack of wild banshees. The town busybody can't help herself. She runs to see what the fuss is all about.

"Warren? Donna? What are you doing causing all this racket? Is that blood? This had better not be one of your tricks."

Betty charges out of the house leaving me behind with an unsigned policy and the sweater, or "the sweeter." I have no choice but to follow. When we catch up to the hooligans in the town center, it's clear that this is no Halloween prank. Blood is dripping from the wounds of these terror-stricken pre-teens. Others are shaking with panic and shock. A crowd gathers round to try to get a sense of what's happened. Officer Clarke is on the job, calming down one of the boys.

"Warren, I want you to take a big breath, and tell me what happened."

"Birds, a million of 'em. They attacked me for no reason!"

I look down the road to see a flock of crows sitting atop a telephone pole. I'm not sure if it's the same flock that announced my arrival earlier this morning, but they look peaceful enough at the moment. Meanwhile, that strange lady, Missy, has sidled over to the constable.

"Hubble, maybe we should think about shutting down the festival."

A groan rises from all those within earshot, including Mayor Novak.

"Folks, this festival has been the pride and joy of Elora for fifty years, and we are not shutting it down because one child fell into a barrel and another threw a rock at a bird and got what he deserved."

Most agree with the mayor on this one, but there are whispers of doubt. I generally stay out of local politics and disregard gossip altogether, but I've already witnessed two strange incidents this morning, and I'd be a fool to ignore what's going on. Mainly because you never know how it's going to affect business. Curious, I approach one little girl who is standing off to the side.

"You okay, Sweetheart? Do you want to tell me what happened?"

The girl looks relieved to be able to tell her side of the story to anyone, especially to claim her innocence.

"I didn't throw no rocks. We were like, on the school grounds mindin' our own business ya know, playin' dodge ball, and all of a sudden this bunch of dirty old crows attacks us."

"For no reason?"

"Well, Warren had the ball and he was aiming at Pamela 'cause he likes her, ya know? Then one of 'em starts hoppin' closer and closer and all of a sudden, it flies up an' pecks Warren on the cheek. Arthur gets a rock and throws it at the bird to shoo it away. In defense. *So,* rocks *were* thrown. Warren is all bleedin' and cryin'. Then another couple o' birds go after Gregory, and pretty soon, the whole flock of 'em are on us. We just turned and run. It wasn't our fault, I swear!"

"I'm sure it wasn't," I reply as shades of Alfred Hitchcock's *The Birds* dance in my head. Legends of the crow come to mind in fragments from long-forgotten university lectures. Some cultures believe that a crow flapping its wings signifies an accident about to happen, or that, if you open your door to find a crow, it's a sign of danger. The more superstitious will tell you that the crow signifies death because it's known to circle over road-kill before it descends to eat the remains. I think that over time, the crow has gotten a bum rap. In ancient times, they were actually revered. Norse mythology regarded them as observers of the world. Stories stretch all the way back to the Greek myths about the crow's cousin, the raven. According to legend, the raven was originally a beautiful silver-white bird that had the misfortune of bringing Apollo the news that his human lover, Coronis, had jilted him for a mortal. In a fit of rage, Apollo turned the raven's feathers from snowy-white to soot-black, and from that time on, the crow became a figure of foreboding.

I hear Missy speaking to the mayor now, trying to convince him and the rest of the town, "Percy, you need to reconsider. Something's not right."

"Yeah, you for one." The smart-ass remark comes from the kid I recognize as Betty's son, Zack. He's inserted himself into the crowd, flanked by two other teenagers. One of them is what I'd call stocky, and the other is what I'd call skanky.

Missy ignores the insult and pleads, "At least postpone the school dance tonight. We can always reschedule."

"Are you for real?" barks Stocky. "Halloween is tonight and tonight only. Everything else is just another day."

Skanky backs up her friend, "There's nothing for us to do in this stupid town as it is. You have your pie wars and your big-ass pumpkin contest. What do we have except the dance? You can't take that away. It's the only fun we have."

Officer Clarke gives the three teenagers a stern look as if to say, "Mind your manners." Encouraged by his support, Missy presses on with her plea.

"Hubble, you know I have good instincts. Postpone the rest of the festival a day or two at the most. Give us some time to understand what's going on. Because, sure as hell, something is going on."

"What, Missy?" he replies. "Bruce's dunking and the crow attack occurred at opposite ends of the town and at different times. They're totally unrelated."

The mayor is doing a slow burn over Missy's persistence. In the short time I've been here, I've learned that this festival is probably the biggest event of the year for these people. Good for business, good for public relations, and good for votes. The mayor picks up a pie from a nearby stand and dips his pudgy fingers into it. Then he sticks a thick, gooey gob of blueberry in his mouth and licks the drippings from his fingers.

"Mmmm, good!"

It's no surprise to me which side of the issue this politico is going to come down on. He steps over to the podium and points to the large, glittering trophy. "Come on now, folks. We have a judging to get on with and a trophy to win. Here ya go, Nathan." He hands a greasy ten dollar bill to the merchant everybody calls Big Nathan, aptly named for his size. Then, he passes the remaining pastry around for everyone to taste.

The crowd laughs at the mayor's antics and disperses, much to Missy's chagrin. The three teenagers murmur "freak" and "weirdo" at her as they stomp off. They'll get their dance, but they're none too pleased with the town witch. Now that this new crisis has subsided, I wander over to Betty and give her a gentle reminder of our unfinished business.

"Oh, I almost forgot. I guess we need to take care of that policy," she says.

Music to my ears.

CHAPTER 3

Fifteen minutes later, I've left Betty Trout's home with a signed policy and a check. One appointment, one sale. Not a bad start to the day. My next appointment is in an hour, so I decide to stow my gear at the hotel I'm staying at, The Elora Inn. When I check in, the officious desk clerk makes it his business to give me a short history of their newly-renovated hotel as he hands me my passkey. The inn was erected on the foundations of a gristmill built back in 1833. After the mill closed in 1974 due to economic shifts, it was turned into a hotel to accommodate the bourgeoning tourist business. Over the years, it has struggled and changed hands a number of times until recently, when a foreign investment group rescued it. The new management is very proud of their latest iteration, and when I get to my room, I see why. It features a Jacuzzi-style bathtub, a fireplace, a king size bed, and antique furniture culled from around the countryside. They're marketing this place as a five-star weekend getaway. Darlene would have loved it, which immediately triggers my thirst. It doesn't take long to find the mini bar. It takes even less time to discover there's no liquor in it, only soft drinks and sparkling water at four dollars a bottle. Their prices are five-star as well.

I stare out at the Grand River below my window, trying to quell my craving for a drink. From here, I can see all the way to the falls. Just at its crest is a curious outcropping of trees they call the "Tooth of Time." It's an islet in the middle of the river that somehow has withstood the surging waters for centuries and has become an enduring touchstone to the community. Past the "Tooth," I'm told the water drops over twenty meters into the gorge and travels through a network of river systems that empty into one of the great lakes. Also below my window, is a newly-installed boardwalk that allows visitors a scenic view of the river. I just might find a liquor store and relax out there later with a drink. For now, I'll wander around and get a little exercise before my next appointment.

The first thing the locals impress upon me through our conversations is how important tourism has become to Elora. The summer months allow for all types of outdoor sports including river rafting, swimming in the quarry, and rock climbing. In the winter, they change over to snow-related activities—cross-country skiing and skating. The rest of the year, they fill the calendar with a host of festivals related to reading, music, and food. Somebody drops a hat or kicks a cat and the next thing you know, there's a festival. But most of the talk around town today is over the strange goings-on. It's all traced back to the festival's origins and their rivalry with their neighbor, Fergus, a town that lies about six miles upriver. Both were built on The Grand years ago and relied on it for their livelihood until industry around these parts died off. Hungry for a dollar, it didn't take long for competition between the two villages to take root. It all began quite innocently in the form of an annual harvest celebration. The residents of both towns would put on various contests including who could grow the largest pumpkin, and, of course, who could bake the finest pastries. Petty jealousies sprouted and spread like the plague. Competitions became fierce, even hostile, because the town that could boast the best pies and sausages got the lion's share of the tourist dollars. In those days, it always went to Fergus. Then, about fifty years ago, Elora took the trophy and has kept it ever since. Now, I don't necessarily buy into the fact that it's "in the dirt" like old Titus says, but something certainly happened back then that changed the landscape. I step into one of the tourist shops and purchase a little doll. It's something I like to do whenever I go to a new town. Then I bring it out to my car and put it in the trunk.

"Excuse me, Alexander?"

It's that woman, Missy, again. Damn. She looks at me curiously.

"Yes?"

"Quite a shock what happened to little Bruce this morning, wasn't it?"

"Huh?"

"I noticed you there in the crowd earlier," she says. "Didn't get a chance to introduce myself. I'm Missy Claridge."

She holds out her hand and I shake it. She has a firm, assured grip.

"Nice to meet you, Missy."

"You don't look like one those tourists who comes to 'ooh and ahh' over all the ridiculous Halloween monstrosities. Can I ask your business here in Elora?"

I was worried she was going to question me about the doll, but I'm still a little taken aback. I would expect that if anyone was going to question me like that, it would be an officer of the law, and only if I was acting suspiciously. I don't think I've been acting suspiciously. If anything, this town and everything in it has been suspicious. Still, the more people I can befriend, the better. Who knows, this woman might be the first witch I write a policy for. Rather than getting my back up, I employ my most charming and friendly tone.

"Well Missy, I provide peace of mind."

"In what way?"

"My company, Hale Insurance, makes sure money is available to families not if, but *when* a family member dies, to cover outstanding debts. I find that many people had insurance when they were young but had to cancel it because of economic changes in their lives. We provide insurance for adults no matter what their age or budget so that when they pass away, their children are protected. Do you have children, Missy?"

There's a moment's hesitancy before she speaks.

"Are you pitching me, Mister Malefant?" she chuckles.

I'm beginning to understand why she's so disliked around here. The woman has a way of getting under your skin. I could easily get defensive, but it wouldn't serve my interests or hers, especially if she's considering a plan to protect her offspring.

"I'm not a salesman, Ms. Claridge, I'm a registered licensed insurance agent. I only mention it because, in my experience, the last thing parents want to do is saddle their children with unnecessary debt or funeral costs when they pass."

"Mister Malefant, this morning at the park, did you see anything slip out of that barrel?"

"I beg your pardon? Barrel? I'm not sure what you mean…"

"Oh, I think you do." An awkward silence hangs in the air before she continues, "But you're right, you know. No one wants to leave their children with debt."

"So you'd like me to drop by to explain the plan?"

"Sure."

"Shall we say 7:00 p.m.?"

"Sounds good. Don't forget, it's Halloween. Watch your driving. Children will be everywhere."

"Not to worry. I am the safest driver on the road. Oh, by the way, what's your address?"

"837 Tracey Avenue. Just down that way…"

"I have a GPS, thanks. See you at 7:00, Missy."

I like to repeat a client's name. Not only does it help me remember it, but people love hearing their name. I hold out my hand for Missy to shake again. I'll have to make sure I steer the meeting. Some people have a way of hijacking the conversation and this woman certainly seems capable of it. In fact, as she smiles and walks away, I wonder if I'm the one being manipulated. I hear someone snickering a few feet away, the man they call Big Nathan.

"What?" I ask.

"Nothin', 'cept that crazy bitch doesn't have any kids."

*****

My next appointments start off well, but take unexpected turns. The first conversation goes something like:

"So Ben, which plan might be best for you?"

"I'll think about it."

"What aspects of the plan don't you understand?"

"None."

"So you understand all the aspects of the

plan as I've explained them and you're good with it?"

"Yeah."

"Is the plan too expensive? Because I can show you another…"

"No. I can afford it, I just don't like to rush into anything."

"I understand. But I think what you're really saying is that you don't want to make a decision. Granted, sometimes it's easier not to do anything. But Ben, this problem has been haunting you for seventy-four years. If you don't do something now, then when?"

"I don't wanna be pressured."

"I understand. But I want you to look back at all the times when you did make a decision—whether it was to lose weight, or buy a house, or ask your wife to marry you. Every time you faced your fear and overcame it, that's when your life changed. This is no different. Fear is what's creating the pressure and blocking you from making a decision. That's the problem."

"Okay, I'll solve the problem. How's about if you don't get out of my house right now I'll call the police?"

"Well, at least you've made a decision, haven't you? Thanks for your time."

On the second appointment, I hear one of those stories that leaves me dumbfounded:

"My father had cancer. He was taking chemo and radiation, but nothing was helping so he decided to take the advice of a homeopath. This woman lived in a different town but insisted that distance wasn't a factor. She told my father to take a swab of his mouth, put it in an envelope and send it to her. She would analyze it and recommend a remedy. She charged $100.00 for each session. One time, he ran out of envelopes so she told him to take a swab and put it on a sheet of paper, circle the spot where the saliva was, and fax it to her. She would analyze it that way. Can you imagine? My father eventually died, but not before this woman swindled him out of close to $1,000.00."

Thankfully, my client knew the difference between an insurance agent and a con artist. I wrote her a policy and gave her a big hug.

The next appointment just about broke my heart:

"Hi, Mrs. Martin, thanks for seeing me. Whatever your need is, I'm sure we can help you. Let me ask, how old are you?"

"I'm sixty-three."

"You certainly don't look your age. How many kids?"

"I have two sons and one daughter, all grown up. I don't have much in savings, been living on my disability payments from the government. When my time comes…"

"You want to protect your children against the cost of your funeral?"

"No. One of my sons was married about fourteen years ago, but his wife died six months into the marriage of cancer."

"I'm sorry to hear."

"We knew she had it but they wanted to get married anyway. After she died, my son went into a depression. He lost his job and gained a lotta weight. Now he weighs over 400 pounds and lives downstairs in the basement. He tried to get work, but didn't have the strength or the will to do much laboring. I took him to the doctor, but they won't treat him until he loses weight. And he can't lose weight 'cause he's depressed. Also, between you and me, I think he's got cancer."

"So you'd like to take out an insurance policy if anything happens to you so he won't be left with any of your debts?"

"No. I saved up enough for that. I want to take a policy out on him because I won't be able to rest in my grave unless I know he has one for himself."

"Peace of mind" can take a lot of different forms.

CHAPTER 4

It's 5:00 p.m. and I've got two more appointments before I call it a day. This next one is a married couple, which affords me the opportunity to sign two policies at once. Amanda and Rob Vert are the parents of the boy who suffered the near-drowning earlier today. This could go two ways: the calamity could work in my favor because a brush with death generally brings to mind the precariousness of life. On the other hand, they could be so preoccupied with their son's accident that they might not be able to focus. As I drive over, I turn on the radio and roll down my window to savor the unusually warm evening air.

"Now, nearer home, comes a special announcement from Trenton, New Jersey. It is reported that at 8:50 p.m., a huge, flaming object, believed to be a meteorite, fell on a farm in the neighborhood of Grovers Mill, New Jersey, twenty-two miles from Trenton."

They play *War Of The Worlds* every year on the radio and I always get a kick out of it. This show was so persuasive that back in 1938, when it was first aired, families actually fled their homes to escape the supposed deadly poisonous gas attack, phone lines were jammed by panicked citizens, and police were as confused as the public. Mass hysteria. I love it.

The Vert house is in one of the original subdivisions, a two-storey job with some decent yardage between themselves and their neighbor. All the homes on this crescent are festooned with the typical Halloween decorations—tombstones, cardboard skeletons, and jack-o-lanterns, one house trying to out-do the other. The sky is just beginning to dim, so it won't be long before the streets are swarming with little monsters.

I park my car by the curb and climb out, filled with energy and optimism. It's show time. When I get to the front door, I hear the father's voice from inside.

"Let's move it, kids, before it's time to string up the Christmas lights."

I smile and knock. A moment later, a yappy little dog sounds off. Amanda Vert opens the door and my smile widens. It's "the looker."

"Hi Amanda, I'm Alexander Malefant from Hale Insurance."

She stares at me with complete surprise until a little bell goes off in her head.

"Oh, right. Sorry, we're just getting our kids ready for…"

"…for Halloween, I know. Big night around here."

"Won't you come in, Alexander?"

She opens up and I step inside, past a large bowl of candy.

"What's this little guy's name?" The first thing I learned to do in sales is make friends with the family pet. You win over that little guy and you're halfway to winning over the client. But there's a right way and a wrong way to do it. One of my associates lost a finger during an over-enthusiastic greeting. After that, came the office memo instructing us to extend the hand in a closed fist for the dog to sniff before entering the home. Do not leave any digits out there. The big boss did not want us signing a policy one day and suing our client the next.

"The kids call him Sampson, I call him the pest," replied Amanda. "Rob, that man from the insurance is here."

"Good-looking dog. What breed?" I ask.

"He's a mutt. Kids picked out the ugliest, loudest dog they could find to torture me."

Rob is plunked down in front of the 52-inch television screen in his den. I don't care much for TV anymore. It reminds me too much of all those evenings I used to watch with my wife and daughter at home, curled up on the couch. These days, I have no patience for the idiot box. Besides, being on the road as much as I am, I can't follow anything with a week-to-week storyline or get familiar with a recurring character. My clients, however, rich or poor, all have big-ass screens. Anyway, I poke my head in to introduce myself and keep walking toward the kitchen. If I stand there, he's likely to invite me to sit down and brag about his TV and all its functions. I need to get them both at a table and as far away from any distractions as possible. It will be difficult enough with kids knocking on the door all evening. I notice that the home is furnished in simple but good taste with everything in its place. Even with two kids and a dog, the rugs look spotless, which tells me Amanda is probably a bit of a neat freak.

"You keep a very tidy home, Amanda."

That compliment goes ignored, which tells me this might be a tough sell. I sense Amanda's mind is elsewhere and after the next remark to her husband, I understand why.

"So you think they'll be all right on their own out there tonight?"

With a world-weary sigh, Rob answers, "Hon', shit happens. That thing this morning was just a freak accident. You can believe in fate, or superstition, or tarot card readings if you want. But you gotta let 'em go out and let them have fun. Let kids be kids."

Erin and Bruce race into the kitchen, dressed in their costumes and accompanied by the yelping family pet. But something has gone horribly wrong. Erin is dressed in a pirate costume and Bruce is wearing his sister's princess outfit. Before their parents can object, the children offer an explanation.

"Bruce is cool with it, aren't you, Bruce?"

"Erin promised to give me half her candy if we switched," he adds.

I catch the look of dismay on Rob's face at seeing his son dressed like Ariel from *The Little Mermaid*. Amanda's face, on the other hand, lights up.

"Like you say, Rob. Sometimes you gotta let kids be kids."

I smile at Erin. After the family pet, the children are next on the list to ingratiating yourself with the parents. Erin looks past me, her eyes full of wonder, then she races to the front door.

"Wow! Cool."

Turning around, I see that a thick fog has rolled in over the street. Funny, I didn't notice it before. Must've come in after me. Recalling my high school science, I try to do my best *Bill Nye, The Science Guy* impression for the youngsters, which, hopefully, will impress their folks.

"Hey, kids, did you know there are actually two kinds of fog? The first is what's known as radiation fog. That's when the air is cooled to the point where it can no longer hold all of its moisture. Cool air masses roll in over the warm land at nighttime, turning the water left from the day into fog. The other kind is what they call advection fog where a warm, moist air mass blows over a cold surface."

"Oh," is all I get. I was hoping for at least a "cool."

Amanda smiles, which tells me I've made a positive impression with her. And then something twigs in my mind. Both the air and the ground in Elora have been warm all day, so this fog has no scientific basis for existing. Of course, that makes no difference to the kids who bounce out of the house while their mother shouts after them.

"Erin, watch your brother, don't let him out of your sight. Just around the block now…"

The kids are already halfway down the street, joining their friends. Amanda closes the door with her hand on Sampson's collar while Rob ruminates over his son's costume.

"This could mean some serious therapy down the line, you know," he mutters.

"Oh please, Bruce will have forgotten all about it by tomorrow."

"I meant for me. But why should I be the only one suffering tonight? Your sister called."

By the grimace on Amanda's face, it looks like she might be in for a little mental torture too. Rob smirks while he invites me to sit down at the kitchen table.

"You'll excuse me if the doorbell rings and I have to answer. Halloween, ya know. So, Alexander, what's this all about?"

I smile and take out my binder, hoping there won't be too many interruptions, but before I begin my presentation, Amanda makes a call on her landline. I was right about her. She's the kind of woman who needs to keep a tight rein on her world.

"Hi, you called?" she asks.

"Trick or treat?" Answers the voice on the other end.

"Beg your pardon. Are you talking to me?"

The female voice responds with such a loud, obnoxious cackle that all three of us can hear. Rob shakes his head, knowing this conversation is not going to end well. Next, we hear the sound of crunching like someone biting into hard candy, followed by a man's smarmy laugh. The phrase I heard a couple of hours ago comes to mind, "A little trick, a little treat." And that's when it dawns on me: Amanda Vert and Betty Trout are sisters.

"I know what you're doing, Betty, and who you're doing it with. You are such a tramp!"

Amanda hangs up, seething with anger. She stares at the floor for a moment until she can hold back no longer. "Why does she have this compulsion to play out every tawdry affair in front of me?"

"You know why," Rob replies. "Because she's jealous of what we have and what she lost when Stewart left."

Amanda ponders this for a moment, swallows her bile, and turns back to me with a plastic smile.

"So, Mister Malefant?"

I talk, they relax. Forty-five minutes later, each of them has signed a policy. I feel good and they feel good. I wish them both good health and long life and get up from the table. As I head for the door, I notice that the candy bowl hasn't been touched.

"Thank goodness we got our business done before the little monsters over-ran the neighborhood."

Amanda cocks her head to the side, sensing something feels wrong. "Now that you mention it, there hasn't been a single knock on the door."

Curious, Rob slips past me and goes to the front door, followed by Sampson. When he pokes his head outside, he notices that, except for the thick fog that crept in an hour earlier, the streets are empty.

"Erin? Bruce?" he calls.

Rob comes off as the last person to be overdramatic, so when Amanda and I hear the tremor in his voice and I see him slipping on his shoes, we both get nervous. As soon as we step out onto the front porch, an eerie feeling comes over the three of us—Halloween night, thick fog, empty street. No sign of a child anywhere. On top of that, it's warmer than ever outside.

"Sampson, where are the kids?" asks Rob.

The mutt pricks up its ears but doesn't move. I take that to mean that there's no scent for him to pick up.

"What the hell good are ya?" spits Amanda.

Before I can say, "Freddy Kruger," Rob darts down one side of the crescent with Sampson, while Amanda hurries down the other. As much as I would like to be on my way, I'm compelled to follow the Missus. It's only good manners.

"I'm sure they're fine, having the time of their lives."

My empty words don't even register with Amanda. "Erin? Bruce?" she shouts. The names of the Vert children echo up and down the street, but go unanswered. Amanda rushes over to her neighbor's house and bangs on the door until a middle-aged woman opens up.

"Susan, have you seen my kids?"

"To tell you the truth, Amanda, I haven't had a single customer all night, and to think what I spent on those plastic tombstones, black holly, and glow in the dark skeletons…"

"Screw the decorations, Susan. Look outside. The street's empty."

Susan pokes her head out the door. One by one, other parents open their doors and their faces register the same look of worry and unease. Quickly, the street fills with bewildered adults calling their children's names. Chaos ensues. Amanda pulls out her cell phone and makes a frantic call.

"Betty, you tell Art to get his ass over here immediately!"

As was demonstrated before, Betty has quite the voice and her reply carries all the subtlety of a brick crashing through a window.

"I don't know what you're talking about, Amanda. Art isn't…"

"You tell him *now* or I'll fix it so he'll be shooting blanks with that snub-nose of his for the rest of his life. My kids are missing!"

With her anxiety level mounting by the second, Amanda hangs up and continues down the sidewalk. Again, I have no choice but to follow.

"They could be at a friend's house, couldn't they?" I offer.

"All of them? The whole damn street?"

A moment later, we meet up with Rob, who looks as perplexed as his wife. The street is now abuzz with distressed adults running from house to house, calling their kids' names. These aren't my kids nor do I have any connection to them, but I can relate to their parents' plights, and I feel a stomach-churning nausea start to build. I don't know what to do except to stay out of everybody's way. I'm sure this will get resolved one way or the other. It's not like a street full of children could disappear into the mist. The little bastards are probably hiding out in a field somewhere or in someone's basement hoping to scare the living shit out of their parents. After all, it is Halloween. I check my watch—6:45 p.m.—and remember my 7:00 with Missy Claridge, so I tell the Verts I will call them a little later just to make sure everything is all right. I jog back to my car, turn on the motor, and plug Missy's address into my GPS. As I shift into gear, I notice the parents starting to congregate on the corner, probably to wait for this Art character, whoever he is. I decide to go the other way so it doesn't look as though I'm abandoning the neighborhood–which I am.

CHAPTER 5

Missy's house is a quick four minute drive from the Verts', but it's taken me over ten minutes to get there because the streets are teeming with townsfolk running helter-skelter in search of their offspring. Whatever is going on isn't confined to one block, it's happening everywhere. That stupid Orson Wells hoax comes to mind and I try to reassure myself that's all that's going on here. A big hoax. I have to hand it to them, though. Whoever pulled off this prank did it with military precision. Driving along, I peer into the darkness to see if I can spot a child or two hiding in the bushes, but I see none. I turn into the older section of town tucked in behind the main drag. The homes are larger and the trees are taller. There's a sense of history in this neighborhood. *Is that a good thing or a bad thing?* I wonder.

There are no kids here either, but then I remember something about a school dance. Maybe that's where they are. I take advantage of the warm weather and park my car at the end of Missy's street to get a little exercise before my appointment. With all the driving and sitting that comes with my job, it's good to get in a brisk walk whenever I can–helps me get the juices going for the next meeting.

As I grab my briefcase out of the back seat, three teenagers dressed in costumes come racing by. A Little Bo Peep, a Santa Claus, and the third is a little hard to make out. Thus ends the mystery. Where there are three, there are more. In my view, the problem is not with the kids so much as with the parents who have such little control of their own

lives that they feel the need to oversee every aspect
of their children's. The reality is none of us have
much control. An overambitious business associate
stabs you in the back or a drunk driver slams into
you; there are a thousand different forces out there
working against you every minute of every day.
And if you think you have any control over them,
you're only fooling yourself. If fate decides to
stomp you like a grape, that's it, game over.

The second I climb out of my car, I hear a
cracking sound followed by a few more in quick
succession. The first thing that comes to mind is a
gunshot, but the resonance isn't quite the same. I
jog up the street to investigate and see little white
missiles flying from one side to the other. Now I get
it. Somebody's house is being egged. Big city or
small, kids are all the same. I continue my approach
until I realize that the house being pelted is the one
I'm heading to–Missy's. My first instinct is to
charge up and cuss out the little gangsters, but I
don't want a confrontation and I certainly don't
want to become a target. The smell of egg is off-
putting enough for me, but walking into a client's
home covered in that stink is just plain bad for
business. However, if I do succeed in stopping the
attack, it might help to make the sale.

Before I've decided what action to take, one
of the teenagers sneaks across the street. He's
dressed in a skin-tight, flesh-colored body suit fitted
over his lean, muscular torso. Some kind of super
hero? Drawing closer, I notice that Missy's house is
surrounded by one of those wild gardens with huge
plumes of weeds, grasses, and flowers that form a
veritable curtain around her property. A client of
mine who grew one said it was like having a forest

sanctuary at your doorstep. But the truth was, he had a grow-op going on in his house and did it for privacy. Which begs the question, is there something Missy is hiding back there? In any case, her garden is making it difficult for those eggs to reach their target from across the street, which is probably why that kid is climbing over her picket fence. Now that he's slowed down, I get a better sense of his costume. He looks more like an overgrown baby than a superhero. Once inside her property, he pulls up his mask to navigate his way through the weeds, and I recognize him. It's Betty's son, Zack. My original assessment of the little punk is so spot on that I have to congratulate myself. But now I have a problem. If I confront him, it'll get back to Betty that I ratted out her son and may squelch the deal I wrote for her. Better to wait until they've left. Then I can tell Missy I chased the kids away and I look like a hero. If she asks who they were, I'll just say they wore masks. Besides, I'm a stranger here. I can't be expected to know one hooligan from another.

"Wait till I give you guys the signal," calls Zack just before he disappears into the garden.

"You are so sick!" giggles one of his comrades from across the street.

I know that voice too. It's Zack's girlfriend whom I saw earlier today at the park. And now I understand. This is payback for Missy trying to cancel tonight's Halloween dance.

"Man, this is gonna be good," I hear the third kid say.

A few seconds later, Zack's head pops up over the shrubbery as he mounts the porch steps. He knocks on the door. No answer. He turns back to his friends, and with a smirk, starts banging loudly. They, in turn, creep closer. I'm worried that if Missy opens up, she's going to get one nasty surprise. Zack continues to knock, but there's still no answer. Frustrated, he puts his ear to the door to try to determine if anyone is home. That's when Missy yanks it open and they startle each other.

Eggs plastered all over one's porch and a masked stranger banging on your door are enough to upset anybody, but, I get the feeling that Zack's costume has some added twisted meaning, because Missy becomes so enraged that she tries to grab Zack by the throat. Fortunately for him, his costume is slicker than a snake skin and she can't get a grip on his scrawny frame. To help Zack, his comrades launch another barrage of eggs. One of them hits Missy in the forehead and sends her stumbling back.

"Keep your ugly beak out of our business, ya old witch!" shouts the third kid.

This is too much. Business or no business, I can't stand by and watch somebody getting hurt. I move in to stop the assault, but before I make my presence known, I hear an animal-like growl. It's close enough that it might be coming from inside Missy's garden. It doesn't sound like a wolf or a bobcat. It sounds more like a warning that if I could put into words would say, "Beware my impending wrath." That's when I realize where it's coming from and I shudder. It's coming from Missy. It's such an unearthly, pernicious sound that it scares us all to the core. Zack boots it back through the tall weeds and nearly impales himself on the fence before he stumbles out onto the street. His two cronies meet him, and all three bolt down the road as fast as they can. Oddly, Missy doesn't chase them. She just stands there. Then she points a finger and begins to chant.

"Spirits of the four corners, the winds and the hills…

… hear my voice…

Evil sent must return to those who…"

I can't make out all of it, but it doesn't matter. When Missy finishes, the kids are gone, disappeared! How can that be? I watched them run down the street, looked at Missy, and turned back again. No way did they have time to veer off into a yard or even duck behind a hedge. I must have made some kind of sound myself because Missy suddenly looks in my direction. I sneak back behind a parked car, hoping she hasn't seen me. When she's satisfied the street is empty, she re-enters her house. I lift my head to take another look for the teenagers. There are no signs of them, just a few branches waving in the over-heated night and the sound of crows echoing in the distance.

I need a minute to absorb what I just saw or at least what I think I saw—three teenagers disappearing before my eyes. Did that woman actually do that? My mind turns somersaults trying to make sense out of the incomprehensible. While I'm trying to digest that, a siren blares and a police cruiser comes speeding down the street. I hate that sound. It always turns my blood cold. Instinctively, I jump back as it whizzes by. I catch a glimpse of the driver, Constable Clarke, off to some other misadventure, ignorant, I'm sure, of the one that just occurred here. Following him is a mob of angry villagers surging up the street like a march on Castle Frankenstein. Amanda and her husband,

Rob, lead the throng. Betty walks alongside another officer—some tall, good-looking dude. This must be the infamous sweater-sucking "Art," who has to be a good ten years younger than his sugar mamma. Behind those four are twenty or so overwrought adults, some of whom I recognize from Amanda's street. This has got to be about those missing kids. It's been a long day and all I want to do is go back to my hotel room, but Betty and Amanda see me on their approach and I know that I'll be expected to join them. So I'll fall in like a concerned citizen, learn what I can, and wait for my first opportunity to slip away.

CHAPTER 6

"What's happening? Where is everybody going?" I ask no one in particular.

When we turn the corner, someone points up the road, and I know exactly where we're headed—to the local school. The building is a couple of storeys high with a wide yard that encircles the entire property. The Halloween dance, as I suspected. Titus, the postman, is leaning on the vacant police cruiser parked by the front door. When the mob sees him, they surround the old man and bombard him with questions. He stares drunkenly at everyone through milky eyes, a liquor flask tucked in his hip pocket. I wonder what his drink of choice is. I remind myself to ask him later.

"All right, all right, calm yerselves and I'll tell ya what I know," he says. "I come up here a while ago to give little Gretta Salverson a house key from her mother. When I get here, I seen the dance goin' strong in the gym. The lights are flashin' and the music's blarin'. But when I open the door, there's not a soul there."

"Waddya mean, no one's there?" asks someone.

"Are ya dumb? Don't speak the English? I mean there's a couple o' jackets, some soda cans and cheese doodle wrappers, but that's it."

"You mean the kids were here and then they left?"

"How the hell do I know? Jesus! Didn't I jus' tell you I got here an'…anyways, Hubble pulls up and he went through the buildin', but I'm telling ya, there's no sign of nothin'."

Titus takes another pull from his flask, which only infuriates the parents further.

"Try to stay sober for a minute, Titus," says Betty. "So you say music was playing and the place was deserted? Did you notice anything else inside, or out?"

"Well, yeah."

"Where?"

"Out."

"Jesus Christ! Out where?"

"Out back. That's where Hubble is now–in case you were gonna ask that next."

"Doin' what?"

"Tryin' to solve the next mystery."

"What next mystery?"

"Well, if I could explain it, it wouldn't be a mystery, now would it?" He smiles at having frustrated the group even further. Without another word, the crowd surges past him and heads for the back of the school.

"Step right up, get yer tickets to the Elora Festival Freak Show," he mutters.

I hang back, not so that I can sneak away as I'd originally planned, but because I'm more than a little curious about what's going on around here. And truth be told, I'm starting to fear for these people and their children. Funny, not a single person has thought to enter the gym and look around for himself. They just take this crusty old dude at his word.

"Don't believe me, young fella?" asks Titus, as if reading my mind.

"Of course I do, but some of the others don't. So maybe I ought to check things out—just to prove you right."

Now, I'm not saying I'm smarter than anyone else around here, but I'm not as gullible either. Maybe what this town needs is a fresh perspective, and with that, I head to the front door. No sooner do I enter the building, than I regret my decision. Before me is a long, dimly-lit corridor. Banners advertising tonight's dance dangle listlessly overhead. Spider webs of colorful silly string hang dead in the air. These once festive decorations have become eerie portents. Before I take another step, I ask myself, *What do I expect to find at the end of this hallway? What if the children were abducted by some psycho, and instead of coming up on an empty room, I find some ghastly murder scene? What if the perpetrator is hiding behind a door waiting to pounce on whoever stumbles upon his gruesome business?* For every altruistic reason I can think of for taking these next steps, comes a selfish excuse to turn around and go back the way I came. I think that what I'm afraid of the most is that I've made the decision to get involved. Even though these people mean nothing to me, I am compelled to see this through. Why? And then it occurs to me. *This time,* I have to.

I make my way cautiously down the corridor, accompanied only by the echo of my shoes that reverberate against the hardwood floor. I try to bolster my confidence by envisioning a room full of kids waiting to shout, "Trick or Treat." But with everything I've seen up until now, I seriously doubt it. Perversely, I'm not disappointed when I throw open the gym doors to find nothing but blaring rock music and strobe lights bouncing off the walls.

"Jus' like I said." says a voice behind me.

Titus stands by the entrance with a big,

wide, I-told-you-so grin.

"Closets and classrooms checked out?" I ask.

"I'm tellin' ya, there ain't no one here."

I kneel down to study a crumpled sweatshirt.

"Wouldn't touch anything if I were you, Sherlock," says the old man. "Constable might get pissed you're tampering with his evidence."

He's right again. I get up from my G-Man crouch and point to the only other exit.

"This way to the backyard?"

Titus smiles at my brilliant deduction, and I strut across the room with as much dignity as I can muster. When I step outside, I'm even more confused by what I see. The townsfolk are crowded around a large oak tree that, by its size and girth, looks to be over a hundred years old; everyone is staring up into it in silence. When I get closer, I see what they're so fascinated by—dozens of shoes that hang from its branches. I want to get a better look, but the base of the tree has been circled with yellow police tape. Most everyone respects this boundary except Betty Trout, who tries to sneak under it.

"Sorry, Mrs. Trout," says Deputy Art. "You need to stay behind the police line. This is a crime scene."

"Don't talk to me like I'm some kind of stranger when fifteen minutes ago, you had your hands all over my lifesavers."

I'm not the only one who hears that. Amanda gives her sister the stink eye, but Betty has no shame.

"What're all those running shoes doing up in the tree, and where is my son?" she demands.

Meanwhile, the deputy's "crime scene"

phrase has surged through the crowd like a rogue wave. The constable gives his junior officer a disparaging look while gently but firmly easing Betty back behind the line.

"Everybody, this is not a crime scene. As of this moment, no crime has been committed. We're just assessing the situation."

But his backtracking does nothing to ease tensions.

"Those look like my Jonah's runners," says one mother.

Others crane their necks to see if they can identify their children's shoes. Questions arise as to whether they actually belong to the children who disappeared and if so, how they could have gotten up so high.

The answer might be with the crows that appear over the schoolyard and land on the branches by the shoes. Did they do this? If not, do they know who did? They know something, that's for sure. If only they could speak. And then, as if answering us, those crows fly over and land in the nearby branches.

"What the hell is that flock of crows up to?" asks one parent.

"*Murder* of crows," corrects Missy.

I had no idea she had joined our posse, but there she is, dressed in a big, floppy hat. She must have followed the crowd from her home after they passed it.

"What?" asks the parent.

"You got your flock of geese, herd of elephants, pack of wolves, and murder of crows," she answers.

"I bet you'd know all about that, wouldn't

you?" says Big Nathan accusingly.

"That supposed to mean something, 'murder' of crows?" asks another anxious parent. "You know something we don't? Where are our children?"

"I think you know a lot more about this than what you're saying," Rob Vert adds.

"Why? Because I'm a witch? I thought you didn't believe in magic, Rob," Missy says, "Or maybe you do when it's convenient."

"You don't need to be a witch to harm innocent children," he fires back. "You just need to be crazy. Crazy never needs a reason."

Missy doesn't look the least bit intimidated, worried, or crazy. She's probably lived with this all her life. Nevertheless, Officer Clarke tries to intercede.

"Rob, she's only trying to help, and your badgering is not doing anyone any good."

"Well, then why don't *you* do some good, Constable?" he shouts, "and make her give our kids back?"

"Thanks for your suggestion, always helpful. But if you really want to make yourself useful, why don't you take a few men and do a sweep through the area starting with Victoria Park? When you're finished, follow the fence line down into the gorge. Check out the caves, the beaches, river raft sites, the quarry–everywhere the kids might hang out. You find anything, call me. Understand?"

"If you want my opinion, Rob," says Missy, "I think the shoes are a sign that the kids are coming back."

Rob ignores Missy but contemplates the

constable's suggestion. He's probably wondering if Officer Clarke is just trying to get rid of him, but then he sees the look in his wife's eyes and knows better than to just stand there and argue. He jabs a few of his buddies in the chest and leads them away, "You heard Hubble. I'm in charge."

I have to hand it to Officer Clarke. He's just diffused a volatile situation and turned a mob into a search party. After Rob and the men head off, he approaches the other parents individually and tries to soothe their worries. However it's not long before whispers spread again about Missy Claridge. After what I've seen tonight, they may not be altogether wrong about her. The constable senses their unrest and addresses them.

"Folks, let me remind you, this is Halloween. You've probably been pranked or punk'd, or whatever they're calling it these days. Most likely your children are out there in the fields enjoying a good laugh at your expense, and your husbands will find them sooner or later. The best thing you can do now is go home. Knowing kids, they'll be hungry soon enough and that'll be the first place they go."

The officer tries to conclude on a light note, but it does little to soothe anyone's worries, especially the parents of the youngest and most vulnerable.

"You think our kids all got together to throw their shoes up in those branches and then they headed off bare-footed into the forest?"

"My son's only seven," shouts one mother. "There are animals with teeth out there."

"Where's that Claridge woman? I bet she knows something," barks another.

At the mention of her name, people look around to find Missy gone. The mood quickly turns ugly and someone suggests they go "have a talk" with her. Officer Clarke gives it one more try.

"People, we all need to stay calm. That's the only way we're gonna solve…"

"…sure, it's not like you got kids to worry about," shouts an angry parent.

"The chief is right," chimes in Art. "It's not like there's some chainsaw, massacring killer on the loose." He chuckles over his smartass remark.

That's all the crowd needs. The superstitious lot turns as one and marches out of the school grounds like they're on a witch hunt—literally. Hubble grabs his deputy by the arm and dresses him down. "Art, you cannot treat this town and the people in it as if they were bit characters in a TV sitcom. A good cop has to have compassion for the people he serves. Now, stay here and keep your mouth shut! And while you're not saying anything to anyone, I want you to bag every gum wrapper and cigarette butt inside and out for evidence."

The smart-aleck deputy shrugs and does as he's told, too fearful of losing his job to object. After Constable Clarke heads to his car, old Titus shuffles over to Deputy Art, and, with a wicked grin, offers him a shot from his flask.

"Spirits?"

This is none of my business, but I no longer feel right about keeping the things I saw earlier to myself. Between the missing kids and the anxious parents, I have to say something, so I hurry to catch the cop before he gets to his cruiser.

"Constable Clarke, they're not all gone, the kids I mean. I saw three teenagers myself just a little while ago."

"How long ago? Where?" he asks.

"Fifteen or twenty minutes. In front of Missy's house. On her porch, to be exact."

"Show me some ID," he demands.

"I beg your pardon?"

I don't know why this guy is so irritated with me, I'm just trying to help. But rather than argue with the man and his gun, I fish out my wallet and show him my driver's license. Satisfied, he opens the back door of his car. "Get in."

"Am I under arrest?"

"No. Get in, please."

The last thing I want to do is get into that car. As soon as I do, I regret it. The confining atmosphere coupled with the inherent feeling of despair brings back memories I've tried for years to suppress. Clarke starts his car and we peel off.

"So, Alexander Malefant. What's your business here in Elora?"

I explain that I'm in the insurance business, responding to inquiries from the citizens of his community. Satisfied, he hands me back my license. "All right, Alexander. So tell me exactly what you saw."

It takes me a minute or two to arrange the facts in my head. I have to be careful not to accuse Missy, someone he obviously knows well. More importantly, how do I explain three kids disappearing in front of my eyes without me sounding crazy? I keep it simple, focusing on the three of them pelting Missy's house with eggs and then running away. By the time I've spooled this out, we've arrived at Missy's house. I figure he's going to drop me off and then go in to interrogate her. "Come with me and don't say a word unless I ask you," he orders.

Shit. He's going to confront Missy about those kids with me standing there right in front of her. She's going to realize that I know what she did. And if this cop has any smarts, he's going to realize that I left out a big part of the story and lied to him. Looks like I'm screwed every way I turn. Serves me right for trying to do the right thing.

Clarke opens the gate and leads me through the wild garden. Looks like he's been this way before because he manages to find some flagstones that lead right to her front door. She's probably been in trouble with the police in the past. Missy's front porch is as unkempt as her garden. The wooden floorboards are cracked and peeling. There are two cheap, aluminum chairs that look to be rusted right into the deck. The curtains hanging inside the window are threadbare and faded by sun. It's as if this place gave up the fight years ago. The yellow, eggy streaks only make the place look more decrepit. Why didn't I just go back to my room?

CHAPTER 7

Clarke knocks but there's no answer. Impatiently, he calls her name. He frowns, places his hand on his holster, and snaps off the clip over the trigger. Just before he reaches for the tarnished brass handle, the door opens. Missy is there dressed in a bathrobe with a towel wrapped around her head. She greets the constable with that old Mae West cliché.

"Hubble, is that a gun in your hand or are you just happy to see me?"

"It's a gun, and we need to talk," he replies without a stitch of humor.

Clarke invites himself in and I follow. The house is even gloomier inside than out. The furniture is pockmarked and scarred, the fireplace is loaded with garbage, and there's a plate of half-eaten biscuits sitting on a cheap Formica kitchen set. There's also a distinctive smell of herbs— pungent but not offensive. If she was one of my prospective clients I'd be hard-pressed to offer the woman one of my patented compliments. *Lovely garden you have outside. Perfect for protecting the neighborhood from the sight of this decaying hovel you stole from the seven dwarves after you killed and buried them in your basement.*

I remember Missy saying something about offspring the last time we spoke, but I don't see any evidence of a child living here. Which brings me back to Big Nathan's comment about her being crazy. While the constable looks around, Missy gives me the once-over, probably wondering how I'm involved in all of this.

"Place hasn't changed much except for the egg treatment on your door," Clarke says.

"It's become a holiday tradition, don't ya know," she replies.

Missy hand-dries her hair with the towel and accidentally exposes the bruise on her forehead. "Is that bruise also part of the tradition?" asks Officer Clarke. "Is that why you were wearing that gawd-awful hat back at the school yard?"

"Nothing gets past you, does it? A hundred or so children can go missing in a town without a trace, but you're all about a tiny bruise."

Undeterred, he presses on, "How did that happen, that mark?"

"Hubble, don't you have enough on your plate?" she asks. "And may I ask what Mr. Malefant is doing here?"

"So you know this fella. Can I ask how?"

I count the questions at nine, the answers at one, and the tension at ten.

"We met earlier today when Bruce had his unfortunate…and then we made an appointment for this evening."

"7:00 p.m." I interject. "Sorry about being late, Miss Claridge."

"Appointment for what?" asks the officer.

"Mister Malefant sells insurance and I asked him up to the house to discuss it. That's all," she says.

The constable looks at me questioningly, "So you were on your way here tonight when you saw them?"

"Saw who?" asks Missy.

"The kids," I answer. "Three of them egging your house."

"Where were you when you saw this?" she asks with genuine surprise.

"Missy, this is *my* interview," says Constable Clarke. "So Mister Malefant, where were you standing exactly when you witnessed the assault, and what exactly did you see?"

I sense both he and Missy studying my every word and gesture, ready to defend or attack as need be. The question is, whose friendship would I gain the most from and who would I offend the least? Whatever I say, I have to be careful that my words don't hang me later.

"Well, like I told Officer Clarke here, I was parked down the street just before 7:00 and started walking over when I saw three kids pelting your house with eggs. One of them ran into your yard and began banging on the door. When you opened it, I saw one of those punks from across the street hit you in the head with an egg. Then all three ran off. Together."

"And then?" asks Missy.

This is where I really have to be careful. "And then I saw Officer Clarke drive up the street, past your house. A minute later, that crowd came by and I followed everyone up to the school."

"Is that what happened, Missy?" asks the constable.

Missy hesitates a moment and then nods, "Pretty much."

"Who was it? Who were those kids?" asks the cop.

"Didn't get a good look," she replies.

"Mister Malefant, I know you're new to the town, but did you recognize any of the ones who attacked Ms. Claridge?"

"Well, yes, actually. One of them was Little Bo Peep, another was Santa Claus, and the third was some kind of super hero–Egg Man, I think." I hope I haven't come off sounding too sarcastic. The constable looks a little pissed, but instead of coming after me, he goes after her.

"You said earlier today, Missy, that if we held a dance it would be bad. Why?"

"Yes, and I wanted to thank you for your support, Hubble, you and all the other concerned citizens of Elora," she adds.

"I am not like all the others and you know it. But I am the chief police officer in this county and as such I have a job to do. So anything you can say that might help me find those missing children…"

Missy gazes at the floor as if the answer is hidden in the cracks of her yellowed linoleum. Then she looks up and stares at him with conviction, as if she's on a mission.

"Okay. Today, that incident at the park with Bruce, I saw something, something that slipped out of the barrel with the water."

I inhale the tiniest breath and hope it goes unnoticed. It doesn't. Missy gives me a look and I know I've betrayed myself, but even if I saw what she saw, there's no way I'm going to admit it. The constable would think me as crazy as her.

"I think that's what was holding him under," she continues. "And then there was the crow attack down the street."

She studies Officer Clarke, gauging his reaction to every point as if she's defending herself at a sanity hearing. So far. So good. "I also heard children's voices." Then she finishes with something even stranger, "Not *our* children."

"What do you mean, not *our* children?"

Missy is well aware of what she said and what it implies, but the woman is in full flight and can't hold back. "I know what you're thinking–crazy Missy Claridge, doing what she does best. But I have a theory, Hubble. You remember the fire of '64?"

Hubble cocks his head as if trying to make sense out of her gibberish. "What in Hell has that got to do with…?"

"I'm not sure exactly, except that somehow that tragedy is tied into all of this."

"And you know that, how?"

This is the only time she hesitates. And then she says**, "**Chloe told me."

I thought the statement about the mystery voices was the big one, but judging by the incredulous look on Hubble's face, this is the bomb. Whatever is going on between these two and how this mystery girl, Chloe, fits into it, is none of my business, and frankly, I don't care. I just want to get the hell out of here. I offer my most concerned look and hope I don't come off too patronizingly. "Look, it sounds like you two have a lot to talk about so why don't I…"

I edge my way to the front door when we're interrupted by a commotion outside. It could only be the Angry Villagers. The constable motions for Missy and me to stay where we are, opens the door, then closes it swiftly behind him. She turns to me and I expect, well, I don't know what to expect, exactly. We both kind of stand there in an awkward silence, listening to Officer Clarke trying to cool down the hostile crowd.

"We just want to ask her a few questions,

Hubble," shouts someone.

"You can't protect her jus' 'cause she's your ex," shouts another. "Ya have to treat her like every other guilty party."

"Guilty witch, ya mean," corrects another.

It's not the word "witch" that gets me so much as the "ex." Now, the conversation I'd been privy to over the past few minutes takes on new meaning. This Chloe woman must be a nosy relative, perhaps a female rival, but none of this seems to bother Missy. I suppose she's heard it most of her life.

"So, Alexander," she says, "you were going to drop by originally this evening to talk about insurance."

"I don't know if now is the best time…"

"Sure it is. Give it a go."

I'm used to discussing work in odd places—somebody's apartment while the wife is nursing her newborn, a coffee shop, in the cab of an eighteen-wheeler—but never in a home with an angry mob waiting outside to lynch my client. Perhaps this is not such a bad idea, maybe it's best to try to take our minds off whatever's going on out there. At least when I'm talking business, I'm on solid footing. So I launch into an ad hoc presentation about the benefits of life insurance and she genuinely seems interested, until the conversation start to go wonky.

"Let me ask you something, Alexander. Do *you* have a plan?"

"I beg your pardon?"

"Do you have an insurance plan for your family? Because I'll tell you I once had a man come to my door to try to sell me some pots and pans, and he said he liked the product so much that he bought a set for his own family, which sounded to me like a man who believed in what he was selling. So I'm asking you, if you think this plan is so great, you must have one for your family, am I right?"

"Yes, in fact, I do have a plan for myself and my wife," I reply. "We're both covered in case anything happens."

I was right about her. She's the kind who has a way of hijacking a conversation so I have to keep her on point. I'm hoping that by being forthright I've satisfied her curiosity, but it only leads to more questions.

"As soon as you have children," I add, "insurance is a necessi..."

"Do you have children as well, Mister Malefant?"

"Well, yes."

"How many?"

"A daughter."

"How nice."

"I mean I had a daughter. She died."

"Oh, I'm so sorry. It must be hard for you and your wife."

"Yes, but getting back to your needs..."

Most people would take the hint, but most people aren't Missy.

"Can I ask how long ago, Mister Malefant, she passed?"

"Three years and a bit."

"How did your daughter die?"

"Car accident. But I want to talk about..."

"So tragic when a parent has to bury a child. I can imagine how you must miss her. A loss like that can either strengthen a bond between husband

and wife or…"

"I suppose," I interject, trying desperately to get back on track. "But again, I'm here to talk about you."

"… or tear them apart."

There's a sense of melancholy in Missy's voice that speaks from a deeply personal place, and beyond polite sympathy for me. Before I know it, I find myself responding.

"The truth is, my wife and I are no longer together."

"Ah, such a shame."

"It's for the best. We both had to get on with our lives."

Missy looks at me with such empathy that when she speaks, it's like hearing my own thoughts.

"When something like that happens, you end up mourning the loss of two loved ones, don't you?"

"Yes," is all I can say.

I pride myself on being direct and honest. I enjoy finding a common ground between myself and my client, but I never like to reveal too much of myself, it's not professional. Besides, discussions that run too personal can distract me from my mission which is to develop business. I'm not sure how, but this woman has gotten into my head. Thankfully, Clarke's booming voice saves me from any more intrusive questions. "So if you folks want to do something constructive, I suggest you start a street-by-street search. Don't be barging into people's homes. Just ask questions politely and keep your eyes open. If you see anything suspicious, call the station, hear? They'll get hold of me and I'll take it from there. If you really want to find your kids, that's what I'd do."

The door opens and the constable re-enters, assuring us that the crowd is dispersing and that any imminent danger to Missy has passed. She smiles her thanks but that does nothing to relieve the tension. Worry and concern radiate from the constable. I know he'd like to be done with this, but Missy wants to go another round or two.

"You didn't have to do that, you know. I'm perfectly capable of taking care of myself."

Clarke responds in a soft but authoritative voice, "Do not repeat your story to anyone, you hear?"

"Who would believe me except you? So?"

Hubble looks around the room, afraid to engage her any further. Maybe I'll do him a favor and tie things up for the evening.

"So Missy, why don't I drop by tomorrow around 10 a.m. and we can look into *your* needs a little further?" I suggest.

"Tomorrow will be just fine, Alexander," she says with a lightness in her tone.

With that, the constable opens the door and ushers me out. Under his breath, I hear him mutter, "Missy, Missy. What am I gonna do with you?"

CHAPTER 8

Officer Clarke leads me back through the giant weed garden that ate Milwaukee. I sense there's something on his mind aside from the lost children. If I had to guess, I'd say he's probably brooding over what Missy blurted out about this Chloe girl, whoever she is, but I remind myself it's none of my business. When we get to his cruiser, I notice egg on my shoes and gag.

"Sorry," I say apologetically, "the smell of raw eggs, even the look of them, sets my stomach off."

"Look, Mister Malefant, I don't know that making any more appointments tonight is the best thing. Firstly, you don't look so good. Secondly, talk of death insurance is only going to upset people further. Where are you staying?"

"Elora Mill Inn. And it's not *death* insurance, it's *life* ins…"

"Nice place, the inn. I'd suggest you go back to your room, catch a movie, and get a good night's sleep. See what's what in the morning."

"You're probably right, Officer. The last thing I want to do is upset anyone. I'm sure everything will turn out all right with the kids."

"I'm sure it will," he says. Although neither of us believe it.

Clarke mumbles something about doing a little more field work and leaves me at the curb. My car is down the street where I left it, but there's no way in hell I'm going back to my room right now, I'm too wound up. Exercise has always been a good stress reliever for me, so I decide to walk around until fatigue sets in.

Along the way, I pass one of those pitiful couples searching for their children. The sound of them calling out their kids' names in the dark is positively heartbreaking. There are more on every street, trampling through their neighbors' lots and demanding whatever information they can glean. That's sad enough, but there's a sinister tone creeping into these conversations. In small towns like this, everybody knows everybody else; thus, every question has a tinge of intimidation to it because whoever is responsible for this abduction, whoever is the culprit, is likely to be someone they know. Tensions run high and arguments crackle like sparks from a downed power line. This is not making me feel any better. I notice a number of familiar faces down by the park, so I wander over.

The tables with all the prized foods and baked goods have been left untouched. Beyond them I see a crowd hovering around "The Tall Man" statue. The caption reading, "who's in charge" has never been so prescient. At its base is Mayor Novak, who I'm sure has positioned himself there to draw as much strength and goodwill as he can from it. The mayor assures his constituents that everything that can be done is being done, but it's just a line and everyone knows it. Questions fly at him from every direction, and the poor guy looks like Humpty-Dumpty on the verge of a stroke. The most vocal in the crowd is Big Nathan, who is demanding that Missy Claridge be taken in for questioning.

"I tell you, she knows things. She warned us, didn't she, not to throw that school dance? We all heard."

"Look, Nathan, you don't want us to lock up every Tom, Dick and Harry just for the sake of saying we did something, do ya? 'Cause if that was the goal, I'd just as soon lock *you* up for disturbing the peace. Now, we all want the children back, but we want to find the persons responsible."

"Then get yourself some more boots on the ground," argues Nathan. "Call in the provincial police, the army. Do whatever it takes. Hubble is as useless as a gear shift on a pony. Everybody knows the only reason he got elected is 'cause you and his old man were poker buddies."

Mayor Novak stiffens at the accusation, but as a savvy politician, he's never at a loss for words. "Officer Clarke is very capable and has every available resource out there right now searching for your children. One thing certain is that these kids did not vanish into thin air. In fact, I just got off the phone with Hubble who told me he has some very promising leads." The mayor holds up his cell phone as if to prove it. "So if you good people will allow us to do our jobs…"

With that said, the mayor stalks off in the direction of the flashlight beams that dot the landscape. I'm a little doubtful as to how the mayor could have had a conversation with the constable about any new information from the time I left him at Missy's to the time I walked over here, but that leads me to my next thought: the cell phone. *My* cell phone. I can make a call to someone outside of Elora, someone who might be able to help. Why didn't anyone else think of that, I wonder? Because I'm a friggin' genius, that's why. Maybe a hero to boot. I pull my phone out of my pocket and flip it on. No signal, no power. *How could the mayor reach the constable on his cell phone if I can't use mine?* As Humpty Dumpty disappears into the night, it wouldn't surprise me if he's waddled off to the comfort of his own bed instead of joining the search.

I check my watch for the time. It's an obsession I developed after I began booking appointments on the road. Never wanna be late to an appointment. It reads 7:00 p.m. Odd, that was the hour I was scheduled to meet Missy Claridge. It's gotta be at least thirty minutes since I was at her house. So the phones are broken and my watch has stopped. On top of that, the air keeps getting warmer and stickier. A cold beer would go down good real good about now. I notice the Cellar Pub and Grill across the street and saunter over.

*****

A dozen or so people are sitting there discussing various theories about the disappearance ranging from psychopaths to terrorists to aliens. Of course, when I enter, all heads turn suspiciously to me, and who can blame them? Next to Missy Claridge, I've got to be the most likely suspect, simply by virtue of being the new guy in town. I smile at everyone and take a seat at the counter to show them I have nothing to hide. I try to get the waitress's attention and after serving another customer, she shuffles over. "Angie" is the name on her tag, a skinny spinster with a blonde dye job. I generally greet people by their first name whenever I can, but I'm feeling a little intimidated by all the eyes on me so I keep it low-key.

"Hi there, Miss, what kind of beer do you have?"

"Only one kind–none."

"I thought this was a pub."

"Yep, but the township just voted to go dry. So, no suds."

"Fine, I'll have a coffee."

Angie shuffles back to pour me a cup. It's not long before some of the diners start in on me.

"So, you just get into town today, Mister? Where ya from? What's your business here? Who do you work for? You like children?"

I'm never shy to make conversation because quite often, it can lead to business. But these questions are taking on an increasingly accusatory tone. It seems I can't answer them quickly enough to satisfy my inquisitors, and any hesitation on my part sounds like a dodge. Even my silence is considered an implication. The longer I sit here, the more opportunity these people have to build a case against me, but if I leave, I'll look even more suspicious. Jesus, it's hotter in here than it is outside.

"You ever been in trouble with the law?" someone asks.

There seems to be no escape from this pressure until a stranger walks in. And when I say "stranger," the term doesn't begin to cover it. The fellow has got to be over six feet tall with a pale, narrow face. He is dressed in a white three piece suit and matching shirt. His skin is as pale as his clothes and even his hair is white. He must be an albino. As much attention as he's attracting, he doesn't seem to mind. He just steps right up to the counter like he owns it. Every eyeball in the place is on him, and suddenly, I'm not the number one suspect anymore. Thanks, Mister. The dude smiles at the waitress who hands me my coffee and then forgets I exist.

"Hello, Angie," he says like he's known her all his life, "I'll have a big slice of that delicious-looking pumpkin pie over there."

Angie goes to the crisper and brings back a piece of pie without taking her eyes off the dude. He doesn't reach for the pie. He doesn't take a bite. In fact, the stranger doesn't move. Then I get it. Angie was so flustered that she forgot to give him any cutlery. Embarrassed, she grabs a spoon, fork, knife, and a napkin and slides them along the counter. The fellow dips his fork into the pie while everybody watches. The room is as quiet as church on Thursday. He takes a bite and a smile creeps across his face as if he's tasted a slice of Heaven.

"Uh, like some coffee with that, Mister?" asks Angie.

"Ely," he says. "Please and thanks."

I ask Angie for a slice of pie too. Only after she's poured the mysterious stranger his coffee does she bring me my mine. She and everybody else in room are fascinated with this guy. It's like he's put a spell over them. And then a funny thing happens: just before Ely picks up another mouthful of pie, he smiles *at me*. I've never seen this guy before in my life. I don't know why, but all I can think to do is return the favor.

"Sorry, do I know you?" I ask.

He smiles but ignores my question. Then he asks the waitress, "Excuse me, Angie. Could you turn the channel on the radio?"

"To what?"

"Anything else, thanks."

Angie shrugs, goes to the back of the restaurant, and changes the station as she's told.

Then the stranger turns back to me, "You were saying?"

"Nothing, it's just that you looked at me in a way that I thought that you knew me."

"Do you like this music?"

"I could take it or leave it."

"Angie, sorry to bother, but could you give it one more turn?" the stranger asks again.

"Last time, Mister. This ain't no discotheque."

Angie goes back to the radio and turns the channel once more.

"Does that appeal to you more?" he asks me.

"Like I said, I don't really…sure it's fine." *Why start an argument?*

"You know what I find fascinating? We all have such different tastes in music. And this machine, this radio, has a hundred stations to cater to us all. You turn on one station to listen to your favorite music while someone down the road is listening to a different radio signal altogether."

"Point being?"

"The point is that one little box is capable of picking up so many different frequencies at the same time."

"It's kind of old technology, Ely." I answer.

I don't know much about albinos, but I'm pretty sure their condition is not a product of inbreeding. However, in this guy's case…As if objecting to my thought, I hear the caw of a dozen crows that are sitting outside the pub on a railing. This is getting too creepy. If I was smart, I'd listen to my gut. Leave this town and come back another time when all the weirdness has blown over. In fact…

I take a gulp of coffee, leave some cash at the counter, and exit the restaurant. I don't need the headache or the commissions that badly. I've been one of the company's top agents since I hit the road three years ago. Even won a trip to the Bahamas. Five star hotel, golf, horseback riding—the whole deal. I remember asking Darlene after we split up if she wanted to come along, but she wouldn't. After the accident, it all fell apart. I've always hoped that given enough time…Anyway, I step out onto the sidewalk and stroll back to my car. With my mind made up, I head back to my car. *Who's that up ahead? Oh no, it's that crazy lady, Missy. What's that psycho up to now?* She's got her ear pressed up against a storefront window like she's listening in on some private conversation. The more I encounter this woman, the less I like her. In fact, the more I get to know this whole town…Now she's speaking to it, arguing with it. Oh my god! What is that? It looks like something inside the glass is reaching out to her. My instincts tell me to keep on walking, to mind my own business, but the look on her face, it's like the look on Darlene's face that night.

"Ms. Claridge? Missy? Are you okay?"

I'm only twenty feet away. I know she can hear me. Now it looks like whatever has got her is pulling her in. Are my eyes playing tricks on me? Her hands are actually sinking into the glass. How can that be? I run over and grab Missy around the waist. Her body stiffens at my touch, but no matter how hard I pull, I can't budge her. I'm yelling at her but she's oblivious to me. I tighten on her so firmly that my eyes clench shut, but still nothing. I force my eyes open to see what the hell has got hold of her, and that's when I see them–arms, dozens of them, reaching out from *inside* the window, pulling her in.

"Please stop," she says.

"Don't worry, I'm going to help you," I reply.

"I'm sorry…" she whimpers. "…I'm trying."

Who is she talking to, me or to someone else? I look over her shoulder and that's when I see faces of angry children looking out from *inside* the glass. There's something familiar about them, I can't put my finger on it. And then it comes to me—these apparitions have the same milky consistency as the thing that grabbed Bruce earlier this morning and slithered into the ground. They're staring at me now like they're pissed, but I'm not letting go. I give Missy one big jerk, and we both fall back onto the pavement as the window pane breaks and shatters all around us. Pain ripples through my forearms. I've either cut myself on some broken shards or scraped myself on the sidewalk, but at least I've saved her.

"What did you do that for?" Missy says as she gets to her feet. "I had everything under control."

"Are you kidding me? You were being pulled into that mirror by some kind of…I dunno what."

"You should've minded your own business."

"You're welcome," I mutter as I get to my feet and check my cuts. She's right. I should have just kept on going.

"Who were they?" I ask.

She turns with surprise. "You saw them, Mister Malefant?"

"Of course. They had you by the arm. They were….oh God, are those the missing kids everybody's looking for?"

"No." she says flatly. "Those are the others."

"The others? The other what?"

Before she can explain, a light pops on inside the store. The front door opens and Big Nathan rushes out, shouting at the top of his lungs, "My window! What the hell didja do to my window, you crazy bitch?"

"Owe!" I screech. Missy has just pulled a sliver of glass out of my forearm.

"Sorry. It was an accident," she says to me as much as to him.

"Oh praise be to the lord it wasn't on purpose," replies Nathan, his voice dripping with sarcasm. Then he looks at me. "Who are you, the new boyfriend?" Before I can answer, he shouts, "Where's a cop when you need him?"

"Last time I saw the constable," I reply, "He was going off into the fields to search for the children."

"Then let's go find him. All three of us."

He grabs us by the collar with his meaty hands and pushes us down the street. Great. Every time I try to do the right thing, it turns around and bites me in the ass.

*****

As we march along, Missy whispers, "You gonna tell 'em what you saw, Alex?"

"I don't know. I mean, I don't know exactly what it is I did see, Miss Claridge."

"You're not going to say anything. All you're interested in is protecting yourself. I know you saw what I saw—twice today–first, when Bruce

73

was held under water and just now. It's kind of a talent you've nurtured, this avoidance of the truth, isn't it? What else are you hiding?"

"Lady, you know nothing about me so don't pretend you do. I don't lie. I am a professionally licensed life insurance agent, and I have a code of ethics I'm bound by."

"I'm not talking about lying. I'm talking about not telling the truth."

"You know what I think, Miss Claridge? I think the things they say about you may not be so far off the mark."

"Well, let's see…to Bruce's parents, I'm a witch because they don't know how I know the things I do. To little Bruce, I'm a hero because I saved him from a drowning. Do you know what I am to you, Mister Malefant? The mirror of your intended misdirection."

"What the hell does that even mean?"

"It means we are all mirrors for each other. In them we see our own shortcomings, our desires, our fears. You're lashing out at me because you can't bear to see your sins staring back at you through my eyes."

"What sins? You're crazy."

"What are you afraid of, Mr. Malefant? What are you hiding?"

"You're the one that's hiding something, Lady. You and this whole town."

"What really brought you to Elora? Chance, coincidence, fate?"

"Lady, if you want to play shrink, why don't you hang a shingle out there in the forest and give advice to the squirrels, because you're certifiably nuts."

"Shuddup, the both of you," shouts Big Nathan.

I've been so engrossed in our argument that I've forgotten all about him. When I look around to get my bearings, I realize we've been led into the town center. Deputy Art is off to the side arguing with the Trout sisters. Whatever it's about, it's obvious the kid is out of his league. Fat lot of good it's going to do Nathan to bring us to Deputy Dufus. He can't even handle two squabbling women. Then I see Constable Clarke turning the corner, and I know I'm in for a real confrontation. The last time I saw him, he virtually ordered me confined to my room. He's not going to go easy on me now. Still, I'm not going to risk my reputation by protecting this crazy woman.

"Art," he says, "you do what I told you?"

"Every single gum wrapper and cancer stick is bagged in your office like you asked. So waddya think? This's like no Halloween prank I ever seen."

Before the officer can comment, Big Nathan drags us before him. "Here's your culprits, Hubble. Caught 'em smashing my storefront window. I want 'em both locked up. And after you've interrogated 'em good and proper, you'll find those kids, trust me."

Officer Clarke looks me square in the eye, "Didn't I tell you to go back to your hotel room?"

That's it. I'm screwed. Until Missy breaks in, "Mister Malefant had nothing to do with it. And I didn't intend to break Nathan's window. It was an accident."

"Accident, my ass," shouts Big Nathan, "These two are in cahoots over my window, the missing brats, and who knows what else."

Nathan's bellowing starts to attract a crowd, and it's not long before the others start to buy into his hysteria. Constable Clarke takes us both aside.

"Mister Malefant, I'm going to give you one more chance, and by that, I mean I want the God's honest truth."

"Well, I was across the street heading back to the inn like you told me to do—it was pretty dark—and I saw Missy standing in front of Nathan's store. It looked like she was stuck or something."

"Stuck on what?"

"On the window. I mean it looked like she was in some sort of distress and couldn't get her hands off the glass. Must've been glue or something. So, I came up behind her and tried to pull her off. That's when the window broke. Look, if I'm partly responsible I will gladly pay my share."

"And that's everything?" he asks.

"God's honest truth. Like I said, I thought she was in trouble so all I tried to do was help."

"What does all that have to do with our children?" says someone.

"We want answers and somebody is going to give 'em to us," says someone else.

Tempers start to flare again. While the crowd is arguing, I whisper to Missy, "You didn't want to say anything about those hands reaching out through the glass or those children's voices?"

"Would you have backed me up?"

"No."

"Then if you think I'd put myself in even more jeopardy, you're crazier than I am."

The woman is exasperating. "What were

those things trying to get you? And what did you mean by 'the others,' and what do they have to do with the missing children? I know you know something."

"Know, what?" asks Officer Clarke, having overheard.

What do I do now? Lie bald-faced to an officer of the law or tell him what I actually saw? Either way, I'm screwed.

"I know where your children are." That startling admission comes from none other than the albino who calmly strolls up in his fancy white suit with his black buttons gleaming like crows eyes. He's carrying that same plate of pie from the restaurant.

"And who the hell who are you?" barks Titus.

"Excellent pie. The best in all four counties. Has been for fifty years so I'm told."

If nothing else, his appearance has distracted the officer from interrogating me for now.

The stranger takes another bite and savors it. I think he's enjoying his moment in the spotlight. "An awful thing to lose a child. A tragedy to lose so many. My name is Ely Shrill. And who might I have the pleasure of addressing?"

"Titus Rathburn, Postmaster," the old man answers gruffly. "And they ain't lost. They bin' stolen. If you know where they are like ya said, you must also know who took 'em."

"Postmaster? A most distinguished position in any community—the deliverer of news, the bearer of tidings, both good and bad. Well, Titus, you can tell the residents of Elora County that the children of this town are not lost. In fact, they are quite safe for the moment."

Angry voices erupt from all directions, "Waddya mean, for the moment?"

"Safe from what?"

"Is this a threat?"

"Is this some kinda' shakedown?"

Until now, Officer Clarke has been hanging back, sizing up this odd fellow. Now, he steps in and takes over the questioning.

"You said you know exactly where they are, Mister Shrill?"

Ely spreads his arms and gestures at the firmament, "Here, there, everywhere around us."

Clarke shakes his head as if he's just been saddled with another "crazy." Do they grow them out here organically? Is that what Titus meant when he said, "it's the dirt?" Everyone around utters a groan, everyone but Missy.

"Can you be more specific, Mister Shrill? Are you saying they're behind a bush? Under that bench?" she asks.

"To be specific, Miss, they are on a different plane."

Some people laugh. But not Missy.

"And how'd they get there?" shouts Amanda.

"Took a buggy ride in one of them Mennonite carriages," shouts some wise-ass.

"So you're saying they're here but we just can't see them?" says Amanda.

"You can't see them because you're not tuned into them."

Now I get what that seemingly nonsensical conversation at the restaurant over radio frequencies was all about.

"You're talkin' about the multiverse," says Deputy Art.

Everyone looks at the deputy as if he's cracked the code. Emboldened, he goes on to explain, "He's talking about alternate realities, an infinite number of them. We're only tuned into our physical plane so we can't see any others. But a lotta' authorities on the subject claim they're there."

"You mean, anybody who's read a comic book," jokes Big Nathan.

"Or papers on quantum physics," says Ely.

"Why are they there, Mister Shrill, the children, I mean?"

"I believe, for safekeeping," he answers in a dead-serious voice.

This gets a mixed reaction. Some chuckle, some gasp, a few just spit on the ground. Not Missy, though. She shudders.

"Safekeeping from what?" asks Constable Clarke.

It doesn't take long for the crowd to grow surly again.

"If that's true, who's responsible for doing this, Mister Shrill? The devil? A witch?"

Ely Shrill's outrageous declarations have done nothing to enlighten us. In fact, if anything, his assertions have only ratcheted up the anxiety level. The constable steps up to Ely who is half a head taller than the officer. The difference in height makes the constable look like he doesn't quite measure up.

"So, what's your angle, what's your price, Mister Shrill, for bringing our children back? You didn't come here for nothing, smartly-dressed fella like yourself. How much do you want? A thousand dollars? A million?"

Ely looks offended, "I don't want anything, Constable. And I never said I had the power to bring them back. I just want to help."

Maybe he's an attention-seeker or maybe he's just not right in the head, but one thing is for sure: the last thing Officer Clarke and this town needs is another mental case running around, adding to the panic.

"Where are you from, Mister Shrill?" asks the officer. "I haven't seen you around before. Can I see some I.D.?"

"I'm from up the river a ways, and I didn't think to bring any identification," he answers. "Didn't think I'd need it."

"And these people don't need any more aggravation or false hope. So thanks for your 'help' but we'll…"

"People generally turn to me as a last resort. I hope when you do, it's not too late." He looks at the crowd and says, "Anyone who wants to talk further, I'll be wetting my beak over at your fine eatery."

With that, the tall, lanky stranger strolls back to the restaurant. It doesn't take long for the crowd to react.

"I wouldn't be lettin' that fella walk away so easy, Hubble. Maybe he's the one who took our kids," says Big Nathan.

"I thought you said Missy took 'em," he replies.

"Don't be an idiot. How could one scrawny woman steal a town full of children?"

"My point exactly," replies the officer.

But Big Nathan refuses to be muzzled, "So

how does this solve my problem, Hubble? What about my window?"

"I don't know about your damn window, Nathan," replies the officer, "but maybe thinking of someone else instead of yourself is a start?"

Big Nathan's face turns beet-red and his fists tighten while the anguished cries from the bewildered parents fill the air.

"Where are my children? I want my children back!"

Surely, Nathan is not comparing the cost of a broken window to a town full of missing children.

"Awe, the insurance will pay for it," he grunts before he storms off.

"One thing's fer sure," says someone, "our kids didn't disappear into thin air."

With the grouchy bear gone, Clarke turns back to us, "Listen, I got enough on my plate without...whatever issues or disagreements you have between you two, deal with them on your own, you hear?" He turns abruptly and leaves to tend to more pressing business.

I'm off the hook for the moment—with him, not her. Missy's steely-eyed gaze drills into me one more time. "Coward," she fires off and walks away.

I like to think that a lesson can be learned from every experience. So what can I learn from this? That if Ely Shrill can walk into this town, I can walk out—which is exactly what I intend to do.

CHAPTER 9

They can have it, this whole damn place, plough it into the Grand River with a bulldozer and wash it down their famous gorge. I'll just tell head office that I fell ill and had to leave. With all I've been through the past few years, they'll understand. They'll assign me somewhere else next week and I'll never have to see these sorry faces again.

I climb into my car and drive back toward the bridge. *That bitch, Missy Claridge. Who is she to question me about my personal life? If she had any idea what I've been through...* I keep a slow, steady foot on the gas as I motor down Metcalfe Street past the crazies who are still peeking under every bush and shrub, expecting their children to pop out and shout, "Trick or Treat." Sad to say, but they'll learn just like I did. Once somebody is gone, they're gone, and there's nothing you can do to bring them back. They're the lucky ones, the missing. However bad it may be for them, it's twice as hard for the ones they've left behind. We're the ones carrying an impossible burden. Enduring endless hours, days that bleed into nights until light and dark have melted into so many indistinguishable shades of gray. That old adage that time heals all only works for those lucky enough to have acquired dementia or lost their memories altogether. The rest of us are doomed to carrying our ghosts around like a bag of mewling cats.

Onto the bridge, over the river, and I'm out of...

What's that up ahead? A police cruiser

blocking traffic? Here comes that familiar trickle of sweat that travels from the nape of my neck down to my butt. I need to calm down and remind myself that I haven't done anything wrong. This is not my fault, none of it.

I stop the car ten feet or so shy of the cruiser and blink my lights for the officer to let me by, but he doesn't acknowledge. Damn. Now I have to get out of my car and speak to him. As soon as I leave my vehicle, the cop leaves his. Thankfully, it's not the constable but Deputy Dipstick. If I can't talk my way past this halfwit I have no business being in sales.

"Evening Officer. Do you mind moving your cruiser?"

"Sorry. Town's been quarantined."

"Quarantined? Is there some kind of disease or life-threatening illness going 'round?"

"Constable Clarke ordered all exits closed until the kids're found."

This sorry excuse for a cop doesn't even know what the word "quarantine" means.

"But I've got an emergency, Officer."

"What kind of emergency?"

"Car accident. My office just called me. I've gotta get home right away."

That's when I remember my phone doesn't work, but he doesn't know that.

"Your office just called you about a car accident? Involving who?"

"A family member." *Just keep on trucking, Alex. You can do it.*

"Jeez, that's terrible. Your wife? Child?" I nod and mumble in the affirmative.

"Tell you what, which hospital are they at

and I'll use my phone to patch you through."

"Well, that's just it. I don't know. I only got the call to say they were in transit to a hospital."

"Well, where are ya from? I'll contact the local authorities." *The bastard's calling my bluff at every turn.*

"Well see, that's the other problem, Deputy. It didn't happen near our home and the office wasn't specific except to say that by the time I got back to the city, they'd have that information for me. So if you just pull your vehicle back a bit..."

"Wish I could, Boss. Orders, ya know. Tell you what, you get me the officer who called you on the line, and I'll see what I can do."

"I don't have his number."

"You have a redial on your phone, don't you?"

"I don't know if you noticed but the cell phones are not working."

"Then how did you get the call that something happened to your family?"

Shit. As dumb as this guy is...

"I, uh, they left me a message and I didn't get it until just a short time ago."

"Mind if I listen to it?"

"I'd be happy to play it for you but I erased it as soon as I heard it. Got so nervous that I pressed the wrong button."

Deputy Dawg offers a sympathetic shrug and promises to help me out as soon as he can, but for now, his hands are tied. The wise-ass gives me a two-finger salute from the brim of his cap and I have no choice but to turn my car around. I may have to brush up on my sales techniques when I get back to the office.

This can't be the only way out of Elora. I set my GPS for home and follow it to the other side of town. Ten minutes later, I'm at a different bridge that spans the gorge, but there's a truck blocking the entire exit here too. I try one more option but that road is also blocked. It looks like they have the town completely locked down, no way in and no way out. That Ely Shrill character must have walked in 'cause he sure didn't fly in. I drive around a bit to find a place to park when I notice two men standing on the porch of a house. It's Big Nathan and Titus. The big bully looks like he's lacing into the poor old guy. The argument continues a little longer until the oafish brute storms off and Titus enters his house. I'd love to know what went on between those two, but something catches my eye down the street, a flicker of movement…it's a young girl! I stare at her as she runs past my car.

"Hey!"

I make a quick three point turn and put pedal to the metal. She's only a few hundred yards ahead of me, careening in and out of the gloom.

"Stop. I'm not going to hurt you!" I shout.

I'm about to catch her when she turns into a backyard and is gone. Where did she go? People pop up and disappear here like, like I dunno what. In any case, if there's one kid there's gotta be more. What do I do now? What I should do is go back and report the sighting to the constable ASAP, solve their little mystery. They'd probably make me the town hero, give me a reward. Wouldn't that be nice? As I drive back to the center, I know in my gut there'll be no simple answers and my head begins to buzz with questions. *Is this a prank involving every kid in the village or is something more sinister going on? Have the children run away or have they been abducted? And if so, has this one girl gotten free? But if she has, why run away from me? I'm no threat. On the other hand, if she's hiding from me, are they all hiding? And from whom?*

When I return to the main drag there's no sign of the constable. I drive to his office, but it's locked. I don't even bother to go back to the deputy. He'll just think I'm inventing another story so that I can make a break across the bridge. There's gotta be someone else. But who? If I confide in the wrong person, it could get me into more trouble than it's worth. Maybe back at the restaurant someone would know what to do or at least how best to use the information. As soon as I enter, I see that fellow, Ely, sitting at the counter holding court.

"Ice turns to water, water turns to vapor. All three are the same element but in different states, am I right?"

The crowd returns a chorus of, "Right."

"Now, let's say you had an experience yesterday, and today you want to recall it from memory. Might you say the memory contains the same information as that previous experience, just in a different state?"

"Except that it's in your head," answers one of the townies.

"Right. The memory of yesterday's experience is like a story in your head waiting for you to tell today. One is manifested on a physical plane, the other, on a metaphysical plane. Both versions are valid, just in different states."

"So what you're saying is our missing

children are like experiences that have been turned into memories. Living on another plane, in a different state?"

"Yes, and that the metaphysical or astral plane has just as much credence as our physical plane."

"So, like, what are we're talkin' here, ghosts?"

I can't take it anymore! "People, listen to what you're all saying. There are no such things as ghosts."

"In your opinion," replies Ely.

"In my opinion, in Constable Clarke's opinion, in the opinion of the entire educated world. These missing kids are flesh and blood and treating their disappearance and whoever is responsible as such, is the only way they're going to be found."

Even as these words pass my lips, visions of ghostly hands reaching through a store window appear in my mind. Then there's the so-called witch who disappeared three teens, and just now, a little girl running down the road who vanished into the ether. This town has got me so befuddled that I don't know what to believe.

Ignoring me, one of the townies poses the next question; "So how do we get 'em back, Mister Shrill, from this astral plane of yours?"

Before he can answer, the door opens and in walks Amanda Vert. The stunning woman doesn't say a word; she just waits for the room to acknowledge her presence. Judging by the way she holds herself, I can see she's used to being the center of attention. I imagine that she's here to speak to Ely, who ironically, keeps his back to her. No doubt he's been expecting someone to take him up on his offer, but he's not going to make the first move. Neither is she. This test of wills does nothing but frustrate everyone in the room. Finally, a few more residents enter behind Amanda and force her hand. She steps up to Ely and taps him gently on the shoulder. He turns as if surprised by her presence. Still, he doesn't say a word, just drinks her in with his eyes and waits for her to open the conversation.

"Mister Shrill, my name is Amanda Vert. I'm one of the mothers of the missing children. I'd just like to say that not everyone in Elora shares the same narrow views as our constable. You said you know where our children are, or at least where they're being held. Maybe you also know how to get them back?"

Ely scans the faces of all the worried residents who hang onto his every word.

"We were talking about that very thing before you came in, Mrs. Vert. Where were your children last seen?"

The room erupts, everyone shouting the whereabouts of his or her child at once. Each parent trying to be heard, each demanding that his child be returned first. I could tell them where I saw one of their kids, but I don't dare now. Besides, it's not like that little girl is waiting there for me. After a few moments, the consensus is that the school dance was where most of the children had gathered or were going to this evening. Ely takes another sip of coffee, lays a few dollars on the counter, and heads out the door followed by every resident. There's a slim-to-nothing chance that this man can help, but the call to action at least gives these poor souls some hope. What the hell, I'll even give him the benefit of the doubt, chiefly because the sooner they get their kids back, the sooner I can get the hell out of here.

When we leave the restaurant, there's an even larger crowd on the street waiting for Ely as if he's the Messiah or something. The tall dude leads his parade of the misbegotten up the avenue, accompanied by Amanda and her husband, Rob. I insert myself into the middle, trying to gather as much information as I can. I notice the constable following quietly at the rear. This is the one man I do want to talk to, the only person I trust to tell about the girl I just saw. But unfortunately, Missy Claridge—the last person I'd confide in—accompanies him. Better to bide my time for now. I wonder why the officer hasn't brought "Big Bird" in for an interrogation. I mean, this stranger arrived just after the kids disappeared, and he acts as though he has inside information. He's vague about where he's from, and with his strange ideas, he'd be at the top of my list of suspects.

I read somewhere that psychos love attention. They'll commit a crime and hover around the scene just to watch the police fumble about for clues. They get a kick out of how clever they think they are. Makes them feel powerful. Maybe the constable is shrewder than I think. Maybe he's watching Ely, hoping he'll give himself away, make some kind of egotistical blunder or stupid mistake. I guess that old cliché, "Keep your friends close and your enemies closer" isn't such a cliché after all, which may be the reason why he's so chummy with Missy.

"So, what was the idea of breaking Nathan's window?" asks Clarke. "More of your premonitions, your magic?"

"You wouldn't know magic, Hubble Clarke, if it turned you into a dog so you could lick your own ass. This man, Ely—I don't like him and I don't trust him."

"First thing we agreed on all night," he replies.

"Maybe all our lives," she answers.

Sounds like some nasty history between these two, not that I care one way or the other. I'm happy to cozy up with my clients so that they feel comfortable with me, but when they start jabbering about everything from their kidney stone attacks to the brother who swindled them out of their parents' inheritance, or when they start digging into my personal business, I close off. As the argument between Missy and the officer degenerates into bitter silence, I tune into Amanda who is quizzing Ely up ahead.

"So you don't think this is a case of someone abducting the children, Mister Shrill?"

"I'm not going to discount your theory entirely, Mrs. Vert. But, how realistic is it that one person could lead a whole town of children away like some Pied Piper? How would that person have corralled them all at once? How would he or she have transported them with not a single person knowing? Was there a truck they were herded into? If so, wouldn't you think at least one or two kids would have gotten away and run for help? There's no tire tracks, no evidence at all."

"So what you're suggesting is a supernatural force at work?"

"As I said, if I were you, I would keep my mind open, consider all my options."

"Elora is a good town, Mister Shrill. Why

would the devil take our children?"

"Call me Ely, Amanda, and I don't know anything for sure except that something powerful has taken hold of this town and it's going to take the combined efforts of everyone in it to set things straight."

I think because of the attention his wife is giving Ely, Rob nudges his way between them. This guy has a jealous streak and I don't blame him. "Yeah, well all I know is, as soon I get my kids back we're putting our place up for sale and moving out of this backwater burg."

A chorus of disgruntled residents echoes his sentiments until they're all silenced by a single, cantankerous voice.

"Yeah, and who's gonna buy yer shitty little homes and move into our shitty little ghost town?" asks Titus.

"You don't know what you're talking about, you old drunk," says Big Nathan. "This is not a ghost town."

"Has been ever since the night we won that cursed trophy. We're just living off the carcass."

That doesn't sit well with Big Nathan, who walks past Titus, knocking him in the shoulder. Unfazed, Titus wipes his nose on his shirtsleeve as if to say his is the final word on the subject.

"What's his problem?" I ask no one in particular.

"They been at each other's throats since forever," answers Betty.

If this mystery isn't solved soon, I'll need to find a route out of Elora one way or the other. The postmaster must know every road, alleyway, and donkey path in and out of the town. Plus, he's the only one who can get his hands on a drink around here. I slip back in the ranks and try to chat him up.

"Titus, hi, I'm Alexander Malefant, Hale Insurance. I saw you this morning at the festival. They say, 'anything you wanna know about Elora, you ask Titus.'"

"They say that, huh?"

"Yesserrie. For instance, down at the pub I heard the town voted to go dry."

"Yep."

"Mind if I ask you where you get yours from?" I ask, pointing to his flask.

"I don't mind ya askin'."

But that's all I get, so I change the subject, "You being the postmaster, I expect you must've lived here a long time."

"Most my life."

"So you know all the roads in and out of Elora. Let me ask you, besides the three main streets, is there any other way out?"

"Beyond hiking it out of the gorge, you mean? No. And why would I tell you even if I knew?"

"Uh, out of courtesy?"

"We got children missin', Mister. You're a stranger here, so why would I be aidin' and abettin' the very person who might be responsible? You know what it is to lose a child?"

"As a matter of fact I do, and I can't believe you're accusing me. I really take offense…"

"I'm Postmaster and I'm old, so I'll accuse anybody I see fit. You don't like it, sue me."

I chalk up the old man's prickly behavior to either the onset of dementia, drunkenness, or both, and slink back into the crowd. A few moments later, we've arrived at the school grounds for our second look.

I can imagine this yard during the daytime teeming with hyperactive children. Tonight though, the deserted school with its darkened windows looks like a building in mourning. And with the harvest moon hanging over it, drenched in fog, the scene could have been painted by Munsch himself.

When we arrive, the chatter dies down as though the crowd is hushing for the second act of a play. The officer, his deputy, and I went through this place just a while ago and came up with nothing, so I don't know what Ely Shrill expects to find. Then, as if on cue, we hear creaking chains in the distance. The mob rushes around back in the hopes that those sounds might be coming from the missing kids. "Trick or Treat," they'll shout, and laugh obnoxiously as we curse with anger and relief. But no such luck. When we get there, it's just the wind that has come swooping down from the surrounding ridge to set the swings in motion. It's an unsettling image, like invisible children at play. Or, are those kids actually there on some parallel astral plane as Ely suggests?

The albino stands at the base of the oak gesturing to Officer Clarke. The constable nods his consent, and the gangly stranger climbs over the tape. I guess the deputy has already gathered all the clues he could find. Ely surveys the ground around him, then lifts his eyes toward the shoes which still dangle from the branches. When we follow his gaze, we notice a flock, no, a murder of crows staring down at us. What are they doing here? What do they have to do with this? Whatever it is, they're not saying. They just sit there in mock silence while

Ely recites strange incantations:

"Oh wise and powerful one, you have chosen this time and place to work your mysteries on these unfortunates who agonize over the loss of their children. Help them understand the meaning of the calamity that has befallen them so that this town and all those in it may heal."

Some people bow their heads in prayer while others, like Rob, openly scoff. "Who the hell is he talking to? Understand what meaning? Like we did something to deserve this?"

I glance around at the other townsfolk who seem divided in their reaction. Some are silent, some giggle with embarrassment, and some make rude remarks. Strangely, Titus is off to the side, weeping. As far as I know he doesn't have a child. Yet he's the one Ely walks over to offer a few reassuring words.

The sobering moment is broken by Amanda who has lost her patience, "So Ely, when do I get my kids back?"

"All in good time, Amanda, all in good time."

Of course, this does nothing to ease her pain or anyone else's.

"The time is now! Do something now," shout back a few in the crowd.

Missy steps over to Officer Clarke and offers her two cents, "This guy is full of shit."

"Maybe," replies the constable. "But he's no dummy. If even one kid turns up, Mister Shrill is a hero. No matter when that may be—tonight, next week, a year from now."

"Zackkk!" shrieks Betty Trout. Her voice is like the grating squeal of someone with their hand caught in a wood chipper. The drama queen points to the ridge where three figures come strolling into view.

"My baby!"

Every single parent cranes their neck, hoping one of the other two youths belong to them. When they get close enough, I recognize the three teenagers as the ones who egged Missy's house and then promptly disappeared before my eyes. Zack, Sally, and Doug shuffle down the road toward the crowd that surges up to greet them. With another joyful shriek, Betty grabs her son and just about squeezes the life out of him.

"Zack, are you all right?" cries Betty.

"A' course I am," answers the teen with a lazy shrug.

"I knew you'd find your way back to me. My love is like a beacon. Thank you, Ely," Betty waves to her big white savior. "God bless you, and God bless Satan too."

As weird as her "blessing" sounds, no one is about to argue the point. They're all too taken with the miraculous return of these three because they're all hoping it will lead to the recovery of their own kids. Who can blame them? I'm a little relieved myself, and not just because I can't wait to leave. I know what it's like to lose a child, the grief that lingers like a cancer, the empty pit that can never be filled. At least there's a chance now, they'll get theirs back. What wouldn't I give for the same opportunity? It doesn't take long before the three teens are assaulted with a barrage of questions. It reminds me of how they pelted Missy's doorstep with eggs. Karma is a bitch.

"What happened? Where were you? Where

are the others, why didn't you call?"

Strange, the teenagers don't seem very affected by all the fuss. They just wait until the crowd settles down, and then Zack replies in a lackadaisical tone, "Everybody, we're fine. There's not much to tell. We jus' kinda blacked out. Now all we wanna do is go home."

His brief statement sounds like one of those wooden responses a celebrity makes when forced to make a public statement. It satisfies no one, especially Missy, who looks more surprised than relieved. Maybe Karma's got its hooks in her too. The teens notice her discomfort and snicker. What's odd is the quality of the sound they make. It reminds me of the sounds I heard just before Big Nathan's window broke—when those phantoms tried to pull Missy into the glass. She glances at me from a few feet away as if reading my mind, as if confirming my suspicions. I refuse to acknowledge her. Sorry, Lady, I don't want any part of this. Still, the woman won't relent, and after she catches my eye, she points to the feet of the three teens. They're all wearing shoes. What the hell does that mean?

Meanwhile, the event has morphed into a cross between a news scrum and an inquisition.

"Zack, I need to know, where are my children?" demands Amanda. "Did you see Bruce and Erin? Tell me. I promise I won't be mad."

Zack remains as stiff and implacable as a cigar store Indian, so Amanda turns her attention toward the other two. Sally responds with a mute smile, leaving Doug, who tosses off a comment, "Like Zack said, there was just us. Can't help ya." As if this will satisfy anyone.

"Don't you be like that, Douglas Sousa,"

shouts Rob. "Our families go to the same church. I know you know something. What are you afraid of? Whatever it is, we'll protect you, but you have to tell us now."

The families of the "returned" encircle their offspring protectively against the Verts and the others who have lost patience. Ironically, the reappearance of the teens is proving to be more of a problem than a solution, and it's threatening to tear the town apart. Missy wants to pull Constable Clarke aside, but he's got his hands full trying to keep the peace. Finally, he separates the teens from the crowd and literally draws a line in the sand with his boot. "Deputy, anybody who crosses this line, you take down their names and I'll arrest them." He escorts the three kids away to speak to them in private. "Sorry, guys, I know how difficult this has been for you, but think how much worse it is for the parents of the other missing children. Now, I know you want to help so, just a few more questions."

This would be an ideal time for me to take my leave. No one would even notice, but something for me has changed. I have genuinely become concerned for these poor people. Even with Missy on my case, no matter how much I want to quit this town, I can't—not until there's a resolution. So I step behind a tree to eavesdrop as best I can.

"Now, where were you exactly?" asks Clarke.

All he gets from the kids are vacant looks.

"Look, this is not just about you. The parents of those children are out of their minds with fear and worry. So you're not going home, not going anywhere until I get answers, understood?"

I want to tell the constable about the child I

saw, but the way people have reacted to these three, I think it's better to keep it to myself for now. The teenagers look at each other, and then Doug finally opens his mouth, "Garbage dump."

"The three of you were at the garbage dump all this time? Why? What were you doing there?"

"'Cause of Missy Claridge, that's why," says Sally with a pissy attitude.

"What happened exactly?"

I'd like to know that myself. Zack steps forward, "We were headed to the school, you know, for the dance, and she just came running out of the house, all crazy-like."

"Why was she all crazy-like, ya think?" asks Clarke.

"I dunno, maybe cause she is?" answers Sally.

Clarke gives the girl a look that says, "One more ignorant crack like that and I'm gonna swat you."

Zack continues, "Anyways, she starts sayin' stuff—casting spells and shit. We was scared so we just ran and hid out at the dump."

Interesting, they say they "ran" and don't mention anything about Missy *sending* them to the dump.

"Casting spells? Lemme ask you something, if you were so afraid of her and her spells, why didn't you go home and tell your parents?"

"We were afraid she'd come after us an' hurt our families," whines Doug, "her being a witch and all."

"This wouldn't have anything to do with the eggs I found all over her front porch, would it?" asks the officer.

Zack and the other two smirk. "Don't know nothing about that except I guess somebody got what was coming to her. Like we said, she came running out ranting and raving, and we took off, is all."

"Did you see any other kids at the dump while you were out there, coming or going?"

All three shrug "No." Something about their attitude is ringing all kinds of alarms with me. Being questioned by the police is unnerving enough. I can attest to that, but these three don't appear to have any fear of the police or of the consequences from their parents. Nor do they seem to give a crap about their own friends. Meanwhile, the angry villagers are growing impatient. The mayor, who has just arrived, takes it upon himself to try to restore calm while grandstanding for his own benefit.

"Mister Shrill, as Mayor of Elora, I want to personally thank you for this miracle and your continued efforts. You will stay on, won't you, until this mystery is solved and each and every child is united with its parent?"

"As long as you need me, Mayor," says Ely.

Mothers and fathers applaud with renewed hope. Meanwhile, the families of the "returned" have become frustrated with all this waiting around, and swarm the constable.

"If it's all right with you, Hubble, my daughter has been through a lot tonight and we just wanna get her home," says Sally's father, leading her away without waiting for a reply. Betty and the other family follow suit. Pretty selfish, if you ask me.

"I'll be by later with more questions."

By the look on Clarke's face, it's clear he doesn't believe a word those kids have said; and by the look on their smarmy faces, they don't care. The three sets of families leave the grounds while the other parents watch with envy, each wishing it was them. Then, an odd thing happens. When the teenagers pass the mayor, Zack turns to him and says, "Nice speech, Stubby." It's a harmless-enough remark, but both Missy and I notice the mayor's face fade to the color of paste when he hears it.

"Art, where's all that refuse from the school?" asks the constable to his underling.

"On your desk, Boss. Just like you asked."

"Everybody," says Clarke, "we're thrilled to have Zack, Sally, and Doug back, but there's still a lot of work to do. I want you to divide yourselves into threes and continue the search. Art, you take Rob and a couple of guys to scour the dump. Lemme know what you find."

"What're you gonna do?"

"Call in reinforcements."

With that, Clarke leaves the grounds. I can see Missy wants to go after him, but his body language implies that he'd rather be left alone to do his job. Missy turns to me and, reluctantly, I feel compelled to fill her in on what I just overheard.

After hearing the teens' version of what took place at her house earlier, she looks me straight in the eye, "You were there tonight when those kids egged my door."

This is framed as a statement rather than a question and I feel the walls begin to close in on me.

"And you saw what happened to them." She pauses and waits for my silent acknowledgment.

100

"You also saw what happened to little Brucey this morning and at Nathan's store tonight."

I know she wants me to acknowledge whatever wrong-headed idea she has rattling around in her brain, but I'm not going to be painted into a corner.

"Look, Miss Claridge, I'm not sure what I saw exactly."

"Don't be a fool, Mister Malefant. And don't take me for one either. There is a reason for everything that's happened here in Elora, and there's a reason why you have been witness to it. So stop thinking about yourself for once and put someone else's needs ahead of yours. Who knows? It may benefit you in the end. Unless there's another reason you're so anxious to leave town?"

"What's that supposed to mean?"

"You tell me. You're in such a God-awful hurry to get out, and I'd like to know why. Me and all the rest of us around here."

"Are you inferring that I had anything to do with those missing kids?" Everything? You were the one who…" She's trying to bait me but I'm not going to be suckered in. Whatever I say to this woman only feeds into her paranoia. I'm not giving her any more ammunition. I cross my arms and purse my lips. Not that that stops her.

"I can't confirm anything myself, but my police officer friend has his suspicions about you and if I give him enough reason…" She knows that with the right word to Constable Clarke, she could have me arrested. I remain resolute. "Look, Alexander, I want to save the children and you want to get home. Why don't we form an alliance? You help me, and I'll help you. How does that sound?"

I nod. It appeases her and buys me some time.

"Okay, then. Time to roll up our sleeves and get at the truth."

CHAPTER 10

The Elora police station is anything but a fortress, certainly nothing approaching a typical urban precinct. Except for the reinforced doors, it looks like an ordinary office with a few filing cabinets, a cork board with some papers tacked onto it, and three desks, each with a phone. A door at the back of the station leads to the lockup, which is currently loaded with files instead of prisoners, making it apparent that this place hasn't had many customers lately. It reminds me of the Mayberry Police Department old Andy Griffith used to run back in the 60s.

When Missy and I enter, we catch Constable Clarke sifting through several large garbage bags. He's wearing a green pair of rubber gloves and handling the contents on a desk as if they were precious artifacts: food wrappers, socks, the odd gym shorts, and cigarette butts. Unfortunately, he doesn't look like he's having much success.

"It's the shoes, Hubble," says Missy categorically.

"What shoes? There are no shoes here."

"Exactly. Tell him, Alexander."

If I back Missy up, Clarke is going to think I'm as crazy as her, which is the last thing I want. I have to be cautious. "I think what Miss Claridge is referring to, Constable, is the fact that back at the schoolyard, we saw a bunch of kids' shoes hanging from the tree branches."

"Yeah, so?" he says.

"Well, when those three teenagers came over that ridge, they were wearing their own shoes."

"Yeah, so?"

Missy continues to connect the dots.

"So they were wearing their shoes when they came by tonight to egg my house."

Missy looks at me and I am obliged to continue, "One of the kids, Douglas, I think his name is, was dressed as Old Saint Nick, Sally as Little Bo Peep, and Zack was dressed as…"

"…a fetus," says Missy.

This time, Clarke does not answer with another, "Yeah, so?"

I think Zack's costume has some significance for the both of them, and acting glib at this point would be imprudent. The officer scratches his head, but not in the way you'd scratch an itch or indicate the person you're speaking to is crazy. It's more of a nervous thing, a "tell." I can see him piecing snippets of information together in his head before he speaks. "It looks like your recollections have miraculously returned, haven't they, Mister Malefant?"

"Well, Missy and I talked, and between the two of us…" I let my voice trail off.

"So what you're saying is, the three who just returned have nothing to do with the kids who went missing. And that the disappearances of the two groups of kids are unrelated?"

Poor Constable Clarke. He looks like someone who's just sat down to a hot plate of spaghetti without a fork and has no idea how to eat it. If life wasn't confounding enough for him already. There's something else brewing here. The tension between these two is as palpable as a fourth entity in the room. I can see him mulling all this around in his head as he reaches for his Rolodex.

"That's not all you've come to tell me, is it?" he mutters cryptically.

Missy chooses her words carefully. "Hubble, this morning at the park, you saved Bruce Vert from the water barrel and good on you for it. But, did you discover the cause, anything inside that barrel?"

"Nope," he answers.

Missy reminds me of someone walking a train trestle knowing the train could come round the bend any minute. "We did. Both of us. And this evening, that incident with Nathan's shop window, Alexander and I both saw something similar to what was at the park this morning."

"Similar in what way?" He finds the number he was searching for and starts to dial it on the phone.

"Hands reaching out, pulling me in, the same kind of hands or digits that held Bruce under water."

"Oh please, Missy," Clarke growls. "How could there be hands inside a barrel with no body attached to them?" There's no answer to the officer's phone call, so he lurches over to the computer and tries to compose an email. I have a sinking feeling as to where that will lead.

"Children's hands, right, Alexander?" Missy goes on. "With the same kind of milky consistency that slid out of that water barrel and into the grass?"

I lower my head, embarrassed over how this might sound to a rational person. "Yes," I say, and she pushes ahead.

"When the three teens came back tonight, they weren't themselves were they, Hubble? You know it and I know it."

"If they weren't themselves, then who the hell were they?"

"They were possessed by the same spirits that held little Bruce Vert under water, the same spirits that reached out through the window to me, the same spirits who are trying to make their way back into Elora as we speak."

"Spirits, huh? You know that how? And don't say what I think you're going to say."

"I am not going to deny the truth anymore, Hubble. I can't."

"The truth as you see it. The truth according to your psychosis."

"What if you're wrong? What if Chloe..."

Until now, none of this has gone well. Whoever the constable has been trying to contact is not answering, and Missy's explanation of invading spirits has been met with scorn. But the mention of this girl, Chloe, sends Clarke into such a rage that he throws the telephone clear across the room. "That's enough, Missy!"

"Listen to me please, Hubble, please," she begs.

"You don't have a daughter and neither do I."

"Yes we do," she replies with conviction.

"There never was a Chloe. You've taken this whole freakin' situation and twisted it to fit your distorted sense of reality. She was never born."

"Doesn't mean she never existed, Hubble. Doesn't mean she never had a soul."

And then I get it–the issue that has been plaguing these two for years. Chloe is not a rival. She's their unborn daughter, the one Missy alluded to when I talked to her about an insurance plan...as if the girl was alive. Oh God, what have I stepped into? Missy has been sucking me into her madness all along. I feel duped, betrayed, and stupid. I need to get out of here. The problem is, if I make the slightest move or utter a sound, I know I'll end up as their target. The best thing I can do is to shut up and hope they ignore me.

"Missy, I can take more than most when you go on about your Mother Earth notions," says the officer, "but the fact that we got pregnant seven years ago and lost the baby, well, I've dealt with it and you need to, because it's become an obsession, a sick obsession that's turning you crazy as bat-shit."

"She speaks to me, Hubble," says Missy in such a plaintive and pitiful voice.

"She doesn't exist! Never did, never will. Get that through your head."

The constable takes a breather to calm his nerves. I feel for the poor guy. I know he doesn't want to hurt her, but he has every right to protect himself from her lunacy. Clarke changes tactics and continues in a softer tone, the kind you'd use to reason with a mentally unbalanced loved one. "Missy, you got ghost hands coming out of windows, children missing with and without their shoes, dead babies talking to you. Don't you see…?"

"All I'm asking, Hubble, is for you to keep an open mind, because that's the only way we're going to figure out what's happening here in our town."

"I'm a cop. I don't work on assumptions based on supernatural gibberish. If I did, they'd fire my ass like that."

"All right, Hubble, have it your way. There never was a Chloe. The sun is shining outside right now, all of those missing children are sitting in their classrooms, and you're not sifting through bags of garbage."

I don't know who to feel sorrier for, the deranged hippie or the man who has to put up with her. It's obvious there was a relationship there years ago when Missy was some kind of healthy, but who could blame Hubble now? I can see in his tortured eyes that he's done everything he could not to have the woman he once loved committed. The amazing thing is that he has any patience left for her at all.

"One more question, Hubble, who is…"

At that moment, Deputy Douche enters and the room goes silent. I press up against the wall and pray he doesn't notice me.

"So how'd that family emergency go, Mister Malefant?" he asks.

Shit.

"What emergency?" asks the constable.

The deputy smirks while he fills his boss in on my lame excuse for trying to leave Elora, and I know that no matter how invisible I try to make myself, the focus has been shifted to me.

"This fella drove up onto the bridge about an hour ago, said his family was in a bad car accident and needed to get home right away."

"I might've stretched the truth a bit, Officer," I confess.

"Mister Malefant, why the sudden urge to leave town?" asks the constable.

"The simple truth is, with what's been going on, I knew there'd be no point in setting any more appointments, so I figured I'd go home and come back again next week."

"I appreciate your *simple* truth, Alexander. So here's mine; no one leaves until all the children are accounted for, is that clear?"

"Yes, Sir. But just so you know, Constable Clarke, I had nothing to do with those missing kids."

"Well that's just it. I don't know for sure, do I?"

This is one of those times when the law is stacked against the innocent. I can always prove what I did, or where I went, or who I spoke to, but what I *didn't* do? That's near impossible. As I mull over this new quandary, the deputy casts a critical eye over the garbage strewn all over the desks, I guess, to make it look as though he's all about the business.

"There's a shitload of shit there, huh? What did we find?"

I'll have to thank him later for distracting the constable. "*We* found nothing as yet. What did you find out there?"

"Dragged my men up and down the road a couple 'o dozen times. We tracked the footprints of those three kids back to the dump like you said, so I guess they were telling the truth. There weren't no other prints there."

"Excuse me, Arthur, was there one set of prints or two?" asks Missy.

"Huh?"

"What I mean is, if those kids were telling the truth, there would be a set of prints going there and another set coming back."

It's an interesting point. If there only one set leading back from the dump, how did they get there? That would imply someone or something put them there. Something otherworldly. Depending on his answer, Missy may be implicating herself. Or is this all for my benefit? In any case, the deputy looks a little befuddled.

"Well, with all due respect, you're not my boss, so I don't have to answer that."

His reply does not sit well with Officer Clarke. "Well, I am your boss and you do have to answer that."

I can see the deputy nervously fumbling for a reply.

"To tell you the truth, the other boys I brought with me were not all that professional and mixed their tracks with the others. So there was no way for me to know. But I did learn something. The telephone lines by the bridge? They're down."

"I guess that explains why my calls aren't getting through. Computers're down too, cell reception, everything. If this was deliberate sabotage, it would be a massive job for anyone. Who the hell could be capable of something like that?"

"Could be crows," the deputy replies.

The constable lifts an eyebrow, "Could be what?"

Art continues, "There was this flock of 'em sitting next to the broken phone lines. I figure maybe they bit through 'em."

"A *murder* of crows," corrects Missy.

"Yeah, thanks again, Ms. Claridge," replies Deputy Dipstick.

Clarke addresses us all with as much authority as he can muster, "Okay, let's get something straight here. A bunch of crows did not compromise every electronic device in this town. Those missing kids did not disappear by magic or hocus-pocus, and their safe return is not going to be engineered by anything but plain, old-fashioned police work." He slips off his plastic gloves and tosses them to his deputy in an effort to get down to business. I'm sure he's also looking for any excuse he can to distance himself from Missy. "Art, I want you to keep going through this pile. Set aside anything that looks suspicious."

Deputy Art frowns over the task in front of him as Officer Clarke grabs his keys. "How do I know what's suspicious and what's not, and where're you going?"

"Over to Fergus to bring Matt and a few of his men back to help with the search. We need more boots on the ground. If I'm lucky, the crows won't have 'attacked' the phone lines over there and I'll be able to call in the provincial police."

"I'd be happy to do that for ya."

The constable ignores his deputy and marches to the door, but before he reaches it, Mary Novak, the mayor's wife, bursts in.

"Hubble, you gotta come quick. Percy's had a stroke or something!"

CHAPTER 11

I have to admit, I hardly noticed Mrs. Novak when I saw her at the festival earlier today. Draped in a formless dress and shawl, she barely registered. She's the kind of woman who strikes me as being more comfortable hiding in the shadow of her husband than standing next to him. I could easily imagine her as a kid, one of those shy types who always did what she was told and grew up mousy and anonymous. All of which makes me wonder why she'd be attracted to a blowhard like Percy Novak? The other thing is, politicians like him generally go for the arm candy. Whatever brought those two together must have been pretty powerful, because they're still together after all these years. I gotta say, I kind of admire that. I might even be a little jealous. Unfortunately, right now, Mary doesn't have her husband to hide behind. She's had to step out of her comfort zone to help the man she loves. I guess in every person's life, there comes a time when they have to face their demons. Standing here with her hair in pointy exclamation marks, dressed in sweats and a pair of scruffy crocs, this looks to be hers.

"What do you mean, Mary? Take a deep breath and explain," says the constable in a professionally detached manner. With all that this man has been through, I gotta give him credit for keeping his cool.

"Percy is…he's sitting on the garage floor, all slack-jawed and bug-eyed," she says as if describing someone on the verge of a nervous breakdown.

"What do you think brought this on?"

"The Dunbar Gang," is all she says.

Whoever this gang is, I can see it holds considerable weight with Constable Clarke, and by the barely-concealed delight on Missy's face, it looks like Mary has just reinforced one of the witch's wild-ass theories. Clarke turns to his deputy and grabs his keys.

"Change of plans, Art. You drive over to Fergus and bring back reinforcements. I'm going to the mayor's house."

"Think that'll do any good?" he replies. "I mean, when's the last time anyone from Fergus did shit for us?"

The glare the deputy gets from his boss is all the answer Art needs. As Deputy Dufus hikes up his belt, he glances at all the refuse he's leaving and smiles to himself, knowing that, for now, he's avoided garbage detail. Officer Clarke escorts Mary out the door as if he's caring for a dotty, old aunt. When he notices Missy and me following, he turns on us.

"Where do you two think you're going?" he asks.

"Hubble, didn't you hear what she said?" asks Missy. "The Dunbar Gang. This is all starting to make sense."

"To you, maybe."

"Dozens of children are missing. Do you want to find out the truth or do you just want to be right?"

"I don't have to come," I offer in my most accommodating voice.

"No, you'll just hightail it out of here the first chance you get." Constable Clarke looks us

113

both in the eye, "You both come with me, you say nothing, you do nothing, hear?"

Missy and I nod and follow him outside to the squad car. The constable opens the door for Mary, who takes the passenger seat while the witch and I climb into the back. The last place I want to be is in a police cruiser again, but I can't let anyone know how it makes me feel. I will myself not to fidget, but I cannot stop the sweat from beading on my forehead. Missy notices my discomfort, so I try to distract her by bringing up an entirely different subject.

"So what's this thing between Elora and Fergus?"

"Stupid old rivalry. You were at the festival today. You saw the feats of strength and baked goods contest. All that began years ago as a friendly competition between the two towns. Fergus always took first prize because they had the bigger population, so more to draw from. The story goes, one year after they won for the umpteenth time, the trophy was stolen and they blamed it on us. A few of their goons came over one night. A fire started that killed the thirty-two children I was talking about earlier."

"Now, Mary," says the constable, "I want you to try to recall everything that led up to Percy's incident, any details you can remember..."

Missy discreetly tries to ask me what my agitation is all about, but I put my finger to my lips, reminding her to respect the constable's orders. She grimaces and remains silent.

"We were getting ready for bed, talking about the awful heat and the tragedy of the missing children and all. I say to him, 'Elora hasn't seen this

114

kind of trouble since way back, you know?' That's when we hear the noise. It sounds like it's coming from the garage downstairs. Percy says it's probably raccoons trying to break in, so he tells me to stay in the bedroom and says he'll be back in a few minutes. Well, I do like he tells me and off he goes to investigate. A few minutes later, I hear some loud banging. I know what he's doing–he'd got hold of a mop handle and a wastebasket and gone into the garage to scare the varmints out. But then there's nothing. Silence. I wait. Still nothing. Fifteen minutes go by without a sound so I go downstairs and…from the main floor we have four or five steps leading from the laundry room into the garage. When I open the door, I look down and there he is sitting on the cement floor staring into space. 'Percy, what is it?' I say. At first, he doesn't answer. Then in the smallest voice, like a little boy's voice, he says, 'The Dunbar Gang. Brad Dunbar, Andy Greco. Doreen Speers. They was just here.'"

Clarke shakes his head, familiar with the names. They may be a legend in these parts, but I need more info to get up to speed so I whisper to Missy, "And these people are who? Gang members of some kind? What did they do, hold illegal beer pong tournaments, traffic in black market pumpkins?" My weak attempt at humor is ignored.

"Stubby, they called him…like when we were kids," Mary says.

Missy cannot stay silent any longer, "What did they want, Mary?"

"Missy!" barks the constable.

"They came for a reason. What did they want?"

Mary ignores the officer's protestations and answers Missy, "He said they wanted to know who started the fire. That's when I knew…it's not like Percy to talk gibberish. He's a very sensible man, not given to seeing ghosts or apparitions. And he's not…crazy either."

As the words spill out of her mouth, Mary disintegrates into fits and sobs. Her husband may not be crazy, but he could be having a stroke or some sort of mental breakdown. It could even be the start of Alzheimer's. I've seen this kind of thing before with clients of mine—couples who have been together thirty or forty years. I generally get the call after the diagnosis. They sit there at the kitchen table while I describe the benefits of having some kind of insurance to cover the cost of the inevitable funeral. I try to avoid the morbid aspects and concentrate on the positive, the availability of money, the comfort of having pre-arrangements made and such. Both smile and listen intently. The wife, the perfectly lucid one, hangs on to every word I say. The husband who has dementia, is oblivious to the meaning of the words, but is just happy to have company. Mercifully, the afflicted one feels no pain. That's reserved for his mate who must plan her spouse's funeral while he sits there holding her hand and smiling. Mary reminds me of one of those poor souls and my heart goes out to her. If her husband has been afflicted, this is just the beginning of her trials.

On our drive over, I notice a familiar house. "That's Titus's place. I saw him and Big Nathan getting into it a little while back."

"Those two have been at each other for forever," says the officer.

116

"Not forever," says Missy. "They used to be best pals. After the fire, that's when things changed between them."

Nothing more is said, no reasons given. Fifteen minutes later, we roll past a set of tall hedges and onto a semi-circular gravel driveway. It's not a mansion by any means, but the two-storey affair looks about right for a mayor of a town this size. When Clarke pulls his cruiser up, I notice a shadowy figure disappearing behind the curtains.

"Mary, why don't you lead the way? He'll be more comfortable seeing you first," says the cop. Then he turns to us and commands, "This is my show, understand?"

Missy and I nod, but I suspect she has no intention of listening. The woman is just not built that way. Mary climbs out of the cruiser and walks to the front door with a shout-out.

"Percy? Percy, it's me."

Before we exit the cruiser, I ask Missy, "Where does this Dunbar Gang fit in? Who are they?"

"Who *were* they, you mean. Three teenagers who lived in the village fifty years ago. They burned to death in the fire."

By the time we've reached the front door, Percy Novak is there in his robe and pajamas. "Mary, where the hell have you been? I've been worried sick. Hubble, thanks for bringing her back. Where did you find her?"

Confused by his insinuation, Mary answers first, "I went to get help, Percy, don't you remember? I said I was going for help after I found you sitting in the garage."

"Found me in the garage? What are you

talking about? And what are those two doing here?" pointing accusingly at Missy and myself.

Clearly, husband and wife have different versions of the incident.

"I'm sorry, Percy, I didn't know what else to do," she answers, bewildered.

Percy looks from the cop to his wife and back again, as if she's the crazy one. It's apparent that Mary generally acquiesces to her husband, but this time, she's worried about his mental health and nothing is going to silence her.

"Percy, you were on the floor mumbling about some nonsense. I was worried so..."

"No, Mary. We were in our bedroom, we heard a noise out in the garage and I went downstairs to check it out. But when I came back to bed you were gone. Don't you remember?" Turning back to us, he demands, "And nobody's answered my question. What are they doing here?"

Constable Clarke steps up. "Missy and Alexander were in my office discussing the missing children when Mary came by. Her first thought was for your safety, so we stopped everything to look in on you. Mind if I check out the garage?"

"Nothing much to see, but if it makes you feel better..." says the mayor as he leads us down the hallway. He takes us into the laundry room and opens the connecting door. Then he flicks the lights on in the garage. The first thing we see is a large red pickup truck with its hood open.

"Were you working on this old truck, Percy?" asks the officer.

The mayor hesitates, "Like I said, I came down to see what the noise was–a few raccoons had gotten in so I made some banging noises and they scurried out. That's all."

"Where? What exit did they use?"

"The side door there, Hubble. Jesus, you forget to take your vitamin D this morning?"

"So the side door was open and that's how they got in? Raccoons. It wasn't ghosts?"

"Wasn't *what*?"

"Mary says you told her the Dunbar Gang was here asking you to help find their killer."

"Constable Clarke, are you nuts? My wife would never say something as asinine as that."

"Not only did she say it, but she said it in front of me and these two witnesses."

The poor woman's eyes well up with tears. Percy stares at his wife as if he's not sure whether or not to throw a net over her.

The constable continues in soft, even tones, "I'm not judging, Percy, if that's what you said you saw. A lot of weird things have been going on around here and at this point, I'll follow up any leads, no matter how far out, because to tell you the truth, going by the book hasn't been working real good for me lately. So any information you can offer, anything you wanna tell me…"

This is a new approach by the constable and Missy seems impressed. For a moment, it looks as if Percy is actually considering the officer's request to open up, until his eyes narrow defensively. "Now you listen to me, Hubble Clarke, you get hold of yourself and do your duty as an officer. No more mumbo-jumbo about ghosts or witches, or, as mayor of this town, I'll have your badge!"

Clarke pauses a moment while he considers a different tack. "Maybe you're right, Mayor. So tell me, what's the hood of your car doing up when you told me you weren't working on it?"

"I didn't say I wasn't working on it."

The constable steps into the garage to examine the truck more closely. "Then is it safe to say you were working on this truck while dressed in your pajamas?" No answer. "Was that before or after the raccoons entered?"

"Before. Before I came up to bed. Mary didn't know that because she only saw me when I came up like I said."

"I remember this old beast," says the officer. "Belonged to your father. Haven't seen it on the road in decades. What, all of a sudden, made you want to crank her up again?" No answer. "What were you working on, specifically? The distributor? Manifold? Frankly, I didn't even know you were mechanically inclined. By the way, Percy, where are your tools?"

"I will not be put under such scrutiny!"

"I'm only doing what you asked—no mumbo-jumbo, just a few simple questions to get a few simple answers. If you can't give me an explanation, then I have to wonder…"

"Get out! Get out of my house this minute!"

"Percy…" cries his wife.

The mayor gives Mary the stink eye, which shuts her up. Then he glares at the cop for having ensnared him. Clarke smiles sympathetically at Mary while she tries to keep her composure. He gestures to Missy and me, and the three of us leave the garage through the side door— the same door the raccoons and the ghosts left by. We walk in silence to his cruiser until Missy pipes up, "Didn't say a word, Hubble, just like you told me."

I'm not sure exactly what was accomplished

here, but it's obvious that one of those two people in that house is either lying or delusional. Still, it doesn't bring us any closer to solving the mysteries around here. When we climb back into the back seat, I have to ask, "So, the Dunbar Gang?"

CHAPTER 12

"They weren't much of a gang to speak of really," explains Clarke. "Just three mischievous kids. I don't know how exactly, but they were involved in a fire at the local school that killed a whole lot of children. There are a number of stories circulating and each one has a different take depending on who's telling it."

It's a ten-minute ride back to town, which gives Missy and the constable enough time to fill me in on the backstory of the tragedy that wouldn't die. It seems that the more we investigate the current mystery of Elora's missing children, the more this old one grows with significance.

"Thirty-two children died that night fifty years ago," adds Missy.

"Fifty years ago tonight to be exact," he adds.

That tidbit of information sends shivers down my spine. "The Dunbar Gang. Did they cause the fire or did they die in the fire?"

"I thought all you wanted was to get out of town, Mister Malefant," the officer says with a smirk.

"Well, as long as we're here. Earlier tonight, you mentioned a few goons from Fergus came over to get their stolen trophy back, that they were the ones who started the fire. So who's to blame: that bunch from Fergus or the Dunbar Gang?"

The constable has driven us back to Metcalfe Street, but for the first time I'm in no hurry to get out of the cruiser. I'm too caught up in what happened all those years ago. Missy is about to launch into her version of the story, but we're interrupted by angry voices from across the street.

The constable grunts his displeasure when he sees more trouble brewing in the park, "What now?" He turns off the motor and orders us out of the car. When we get close enough to the action, I see a mob has encircled Ely.

Big Nathan's bark is the loudest, "Ya don't go waltzing into a town making promises ya can't keep, Mister Shrill. You claim you got powers. Prove it. We'll even pay you. Or if you don't wanna be paid we'll send the money to your favorite charity–Witch Doctors Without Borders, Satan's Little Helpers, Dollars For Demons."

Amanda steps up to defend her new hero, "Nathan, shut up, you big ass. He hasn't asked for money, and no matter what he is or claims to be, he brought three of our kids back, which is more than you did."

"He ain't done nobody any harm," says Titus.

"And he ain't done nobody any good, neither," argues Big Nathan. "Hey, it don't make no difference to me. I don't have no rugrats to worry about."

"Cause no woman could bear your insufferable personality long enough to have any with you," shouts Betty.

"I'm just thinking about you all," says Nathan, letting his argument fizzle. "If Mister Shrill here says he brought those kids back, just tell us how."

"Not with the Lord's help," says Rob Vert. "Not from going to church and praying to the big guy, that's for sure. This man is evil. I can smell it.

Come on, Amanda." Rob takes his wife by the arm, but she's not going anywhere. It's clear that the couple has become as divided as the town.

Ely doesn't seem the least bit upset by all the dissention. In fact, he appears amused and proceeds to answer Rob as if addressing a dimwitted child, "I do not resort to chicanery, Mister Vert. I don't use hypnotism or potions, and there is nothing up my sleeve, evil or otherwise. I am simply a facilitator. I try to fight fear, hostility, and ignorance with reason until there is nothing left to address but the truth."

"And what *is* the truth?" shouts a bystander.

Missy nudges me and whispers that we need to talk. She's still trying to win me over. Serves me right for showing concern. Somebody else pipes up and asks what it's going to take to get the rest of the children back. Everyone hushes to hear Ely's response. What he says is as confounding as it is chilling.

"Before this night is over, each one of you will face your darkest fears. Some of you will conquer them, some won't. Those who do will be rewarded."

"Darkest fears, huh?" says Rob. "Sure sounds like Satan's work to me. Tell me, folks, what if, instead of negotiating with the Devil, this guy is in league with the Devil, and he's leading us all to the gates of Hell?"

Again, Amanda comes to Ely's defense and addresses the crowd, "What have you done, any of you? Nothing, that's what. And why do you all assume it's the Devil at work here?"

"Well, it sure as hell ain't God that's stole our children," says another.

124

"And I wouldn't count on him rescuing them anytime soon either," says a second.

"Ya gotta wonder why, when something like this happens, is God always conspicuously absent?" a third person says. "When is he going to get off his ass and do something for his people?"

Ely fields that question with supreme calm and confidence. "He's not. Because if he did, you'd be using God as a get-out-of-jail card every time you ran up against a problem instead of admitting your own responsibility and doing something about it yourselves."

"Responsibility for what? What did we do? Now it's our fault?"

Poor Rob Vert. His anger and frustration is at its boiling point, and he unloads with everything he's got, "Know what? I'm sick of your bullshit, Mister Shrill! You can't prove you had anything to do with bringing back those other three, and my two little ones are still out there somewhere. Yet here you stand, cock of the walk, with no answers, no solutions—just a mouth full of double-talk. Either do something right now to prove what you say, or we'll do something about you!"

More threats fill the air, polarizing the community. It's not long before some of the rowdier people start pushing the weaker ones around.

Ely raises his hands, "People, I've said what I've come here to say. Whether you listen or not is your choice."

And just like that, Big Bird strolls out of the park.

"Roads are all blocked, Mister Shrill. No one leaves," says Constable Clarke.

"Oh, I wouldn't leave even if I could, Officer Clarke," he replies.

We all watch the mysterious stranger cross the road and stroll into the Elora Mill Inn, where I assume he must be staying. That's when the constable hears a car screech to a stop and turns his attention to the bridge. "What the hell?"

Missy and I follow his gaze. Deputy Art's cruiser is parked at the top of the structure. The constable jogs over, and we follow, thirsty for any information.

"Art, I thought I told to get your ass over to Fergus and bring help."

There is no immediate answer. Through the passenger window, we see the deputy staring into space like he's high or something. Clarke raps on the glass, which startles the kid back to life.

He rolls down his window slowly, "Hey, Hubble. I did. I mean I did exactly like you told me. I drove out of town past the water tower, straight down the road to Fergus. Swear to God. But somehow...I ended up back here."

"Well go out there again, ya fool. You were probably daydreaming about the next piece of tail you had your sights on."

"I was. I mean I did. I mean, this is the second time I drove out and the second time I ended up back here. It's like somethin' doesn't want me to leave."

As the three of them stand there dithering, I notice that, for the first time, the bridge is clear. This is my chance. I make my way discreetly down the street to my car. The deputy was probably smoking a joint or something. How hard can it be to drive in a straight line? It'd be interesting to pull

Deputy Doobie out of his cruiser and make *him* walk a straight line.

I climb into my Honda and start the motor, make a stealthy three point turn, and drive right past the cop, his coked-up deputy, and the witch. In a flash, I'm over the bridge. One right turn and I'm sailing down the highway, free as a bird. I did it! It's still dark, but after a few hundred feet I can make out the sign at the top of the water tower ahead that reads, "ELORA." Fifty feet more and I pass a road sign that says, "THANKS FOR VISITING ELORA, COME BACK SOON." Yeah, sure. Another thirty minutes and this will all be a friggin', foggy, nightmare. Tomorrow morning, I'll report to my office, give 'em a song and dance, and get assigned somewhere else. They don't even question me since the accident. The truth is, they're lucky to have me on the payroll at all after what I've been through. I remember the faces of my associates after it happened. Nothing but doleful looks and awkward sympathies. Sometimes, not even that. Most of my friends didn't know how to act around me and often avoided me altogether. If someone was telling a joke, they'd clam up the moment they saw me coming. I can't really blame them. They say a parent should never have to bury a child. No one can know the depth of that loss unless they've experienced it. Still, losing my daughter was only part of it.

What's that up ahead? Another sign– "WELCOME TO FERGUS COUNTY." Must be joined at the hip, these two, but now I'm starting to feel a little guilty. Maybe I ought to stop in and give them a word about those missing kids. I make out the white FERGUS water tank against the ink-black sky a hundred feet or so ahead. What the hell, I'll make the turn. It doesn't take much to do the right thing. Hmm...they have a bridge over this section of the river too. I guess one town is like the other around these parts. I pull over to the curb to get my bearings, and there's a rap on the window.

"I expect you drove out there to verify what happened to Art."

I turn my head in disbelief to find Constable Clarke standing at my door. Behind him is the same stupid park with the same stupid villagers having the same stupid arguments. I'm back in Elora! How is that possible? I drove in a straight line right down that highway!

"Yes, yes I did, Officer Clarke," I answer dumbly. "He was right."

I must sound as stoned or as dense as the deputy, because the constable shrugs as if he's talking to some cokehead. He takes out his flashlight and shines it into my car.

"What's that back there, Mister Malefant?"

I turn around to see what's caught his eye. "A doll."

"You bought a doll?"

"Yes I did, right here in town. I collect them."

Suspicious, the constable orders me out of the car. "Open you trunk, please."

"Why?"

"Open your trunk."

Shit. I click my key fob that unlocks the trunk. I open it and there they are, dozens of dolls.

"Like I said, Officer. I collect them from every town I visit."

"Or you use them to lure little girls."

"Absolutely not," I answer emphatically. "I have a daughter. I *had* a daughter. She died. I bring her things from time to time."

"Back to her grave, you mean?"

"As a gift, yeah. It helps me cope."

A beat later, we hear squealing tires and turn to see four trucks barreling across the bridge on their way out to the highway. Looks like a few of the others have decided to ignore orders and go for help. Maybe they'll fare better than me.

"It's not a crime to buy gifts is it, Officer Clarke?"

"I've got my eye on you, Mister Malefant. Now, I'm ordering you to go to your hotel room and remain there until I come for you in the morning."

"But I haven't broken any law."

"It's that or jail. You can leave your car right here."

He has no right to confine me to my room or go through my car like I'm a common criminal. In fact, they need me out here to help find the perpetrator and solve the mystery of the missing children. He has no right. Without another word, I grab my suitcase and head to my hotel. Maybe the answer lies in a good night's sleep. With any luck, tomorrow morning I'll wake up and this will all have been a bad, bad dream.

CHAPTER 13

My room is one of sixty-four refurbished suites in this newly-renovated hotel. I've got to hand it to the new management. They did a great job—from the oak and granite fixtures in the lobby, to the refitted rooms, each with a comfy, king size bed. The sinks in the bathroom look to be Italian travertine, the faucets and fixtures are polished chrome, and the original floorboards have been re-sanded and varnished. Darlene would have given this place a five star rating, something she didn't give easily. My wife had impeccable taste. It wasn't that she was picky or constantly on the lookout for flaws, but she lived by a certain standard and demanded the best out of everybody. That was a big source of our troubles. Thank God this is the off season and I could get a decent rate. Five star or not, all I want to do is crawl under the covers and go to sleep, but this is the worst time of day for me. Sleep has become as elusive as absolution from an unpardonable crime.

My friends and colleagues say I'm a people person, but the truth is that's only because I hate being alone. I need to keep myself busy until I'm dog-tired. I fill my day with appointments and use the late hours to enter my business online and go over my reports. Only then can I escape into sleep. But there's been precious little business today, and even with all the strange goings-on around here, I have not yet exhausted myself.

What time is it? Oh, right. 7:00. Again. Still. Funny, when I look closely at my watch I see the second hand still turning. Fifteen, thirty, sixty seconds go by, but the minute hand remains in place. For a moment, I wonder whether it's the minute hand that's stuck, or time itself. This phenomenon probably has something to do with the magnetic component of the land. I've seen my GPS go wonky sometimes when travelling through various parts of the province. Maybe it's something in the soil—or the dirt, like Titus says.

I turn on my laptop only to find that the Internet is down here too. I try the TV—no signal. This town is cut off from all communication with the outside world, and it looks like I am too. I'm pretty good at busying myself with work until sleep overtakes me, but with no distractions, the walls feel like they're closing in and I get the jitters. I rush to the window to get some fresh air, but it does little to prevent those awful memories from flooding back. I can almost see them drifting over the river toward my room, like ghosts. Will I never be free?

Someone knocks at the door. Not my door, the one next to me. Is it Constable Clarke? No, I hear a woman's voice calling out—someone I recognize. I'm not a nosy guy by nature but thank God for the diversion. I tiptoe to my front door and crack it open. She's standing just down the hall.

"Mister Shrill, it's Amanda Vert. May I speak with you?"

She's changed her dress to a pretty emerald green number. Through the opening, I watch her adjust her shoulder straps to better show off her cleavage.

The door opens.

"I see they're treating you well," she says.

"The people of Elora have been very good to

me, thank you, Mrs. Vert," says Ely, swallowing a bite of apple. This guy is always eating.

"As they should be. They're lucky to have you. Do you have a minute, Mister Shrill? May I come in, Ely?"

The door squeaks open and she vanishes into his room. What is she up to? Not that I care what she does personally, but there's no way she's here on behalf of the welcome wagon. I pad over to the connecting door that adjoins our rooms to eavesdrop. All is quiet for the moment. They're probably sizing each other up, figuring out who wants what, and what this is going to cost each of them.

"So you never told me, Ely, where you're from."

No answer.

"My, how mysterious we are," she murmurs. "I don't know if I like that or not."

Isn't she the coquette?

"There is something about you though, Ely, beyond your obvious flair for dress. It's the way you carry yourself, I think. And the things you know, although you can be a little stingy with it at times. Not me, I'm not stingy with it at all. There's a saying that goes, 'Knowledge is a sword and wisdom is in knowing how to wield it'. Do you know how to wield that sword of yours, Mister Shrill?"

Then the sound of clothes rustling. I imagine she's leaning into him, kissing him. I hear her moan just a little.

"Not bad after two kids, are they? Wanna touch 'em?" she purrs.

I can almost see him lifting the straps of that

little green dress off her smooth, round shoulders to reveal her breasts. I don't know about him, but I sure wanna touch 'em.

"Anything you want, Ely," she says, "Anything. And then after, you'll bring my children back to me just like you did for my sister, right?"

There are more moans, more promises. I hear nothing from Ely, but it doesn't matter. It's all so predictable and tawdry. She'll use what she has to get what she wants. He'll make her some empty promise and forget all about it tomorrow.

Then, unexpectedly, he speaks, "It kills you, doesn't it, that Betty's son is back and your children aren't?"

All sounds of passion cease. I gotta say, I'm blown away by his response, and even a little impressed. I can just imagine the befuddled look on that woman's face.

"What? No!" she says.

"The competition between you two has been going on for years–who was daddy's favourite, who could attract the handsomest men, who was the best lover, who could have the most lovers..."

"You're treading on dangerous..." Then she catches herself, "I mean, whatever stories you've heard about me, Ely, you've been sadly misinformed. I'm here tonight because I need a man. A man like you."

Don't fall for her bullshit, Ely, don't fall for it.

"This is not a competition, Amanda. Besides, sleeping with me wouldn't be much of a sacrifice for you, or any way to prove your love and devotion to your family, would it?"

"How dare you!"

"I appreciate you're not used to being turned down. You think this is the solution, but what about tomorrow?"

"I don't care about tomorrow or how I'll feel a hundred tomorrows from now. I'll do anything to get my children back, and I'm not ashamed of it."

"That, I can see."

"Look, Mister Shrill, I've made you a proposition—a pretty good one by standards around these parts. If that's not good enough, then tell me what it is you want."

"I want you to face who you are."

"I know who I am, and I know who you are—a pig!" Her insult is followed by a slap across his face.

"Have a good night, Mrs. Vert," he says calmly.

The door to Ely's hotel room flies open, and I hurry over to open mine. There she is, frozen in the hallway, her face a mask of bewilderment and humiliation. Probably wondering how her plan went so horribly awry. Ely was right about one thing—Amanda is not used to being turned down. She shrugs her dress back on and straightens her shoulders with as much dignity as she can muster. That's when she notices me and turns, "You think you're in a position to judge me? Look at you, hiding behind that door. Coward!"

She storms past me toward the stairwell. I don't know if she's more pissed at having been rejected or knowing I was party to her indiscretion. Funny, a second ago, I was cheering for her undoing. Now I feel sorry for her. What would I do in her place? What would I sacrifice for my family?

The passion play has died down in the

hallway, but something catches my attention outside my window—the sound of trucks lumbering over the bridge. Maybe those townspeople got the help they went after. Nope, the same vehicles are returning. I watch the locals climb out of their cabs and slam the doors behind them in frustration.

"I dunno, Danny. We headed straight out on Wellington, drove down that highway, and ended up back here. How in hell is that possible?"

"Because you're a dumbass, that's how. Nobody start offs at point A and ends up at point A again."

"Unless they're goin' in a circle."

"Or stuck in the same place."

I rub my weary eyes and pinch the bridge of my nose. The little drama that played out over the last few minutes has, thankfully, drained me of all my remaining energy. With any luck, I'll be able to climb into bed and shut down my brain. The gremlins will have to wait for another night. The view outside is calming, the river smooth and tranquil. Its waters below gently lap up against the boardwalk, and I feel myself giving into its sleepy rhythm. That's when I see her—the little girl from earlier this evening, standing below, looking straight up at me.

"You! Stay right there, don't move!"

She remains in her spot like I told her to—for the moment. My heart thumps like a hammer as I race to the door.

CHAPTER 14

Ely must have heard me, because he sticks his head out of his room as I hurry past. He doesn't bother to ask what I'm doing or where I'm going, and I'm not stopping to tell him. This time, I'm determined to catch the little truant. When I get to the end of the hallway, I leap down the stairs two-by-two and fly past Amanda, who is just making her way out of the lobby. I'm sure she's wondering how much of her escapade I was privy to, but I've lost all interest in her. The sight of that little waif has filled me with adrenaline. I crash through the main doors only to find I'm on the wrong side of the hotel. I race around the other side to where the boardwalk meets the water, but, big surprise, the girl is gone.

"Hello?" My shouting is followed by a hacking cough. Three years ago, a jog like this wouldn't have fazed me, but ever since the accident, I've lost all desire for exercise. As a result, my lungs are now screaming for oxygen. Still, I can't stop. I summon the strength and lumber around the building again, looking as awkward, I'm sure, as Quasimodo. When I turn the corner, I find a lone figure sitting on a bench by the cobblestone walkway. It's not the girl. It's Missy Claridge.

"Alexander, what's wrong?" She asks.

Breathless, I can barely make myself understood. "Girl...outside my window...boardwalk. Did...see her?" The question mark in Missy's eyes gives me the answer. Another gasp or two and I resume my search. I want to find this girl. I *need* to find her.

"What girl? What did she look like?" Missy fires off a half dozen annoying questions as she follows me around the building—none of which I have the patience or the breath to answer.

I continue along the boardwalk until I stop just below my hotel window. I've covered this area twice. If the kid was there at all, she's long gone now. I'm starting to think that I've imagined her, or worse, that my mind has begun that dreaded descent that so many of my clients have slipped into. I'm going to end up crazy and alone.

Then, I hear Missy call me, "Alexander." I follow her gaze to an outcropping of trees rooted in the middle of the river by the edge of the falls—The Tooth of Time. There she is–the girl I saw on the bridge earlier tonight, the same girl who stood below my window a few minutes ago. It's too dark and distant to make out her face, but she's there all right, standing amid the foliage as the water churns and bubbles around her.

"You see her?" I manage to ask. Missy nods. Tears pool in my eyes. I'm not crazy. Right now, I could kiss the woman. "How could she get out there?"

It's such an improbable sight that we're both afraid to make a sound for fear she'll disappear. Though, where would she go, trapped on that tiny islet? The girl acknowledges us with a look and, without saying a word, turns her back before she walks out of sight into the trees. I feel my teeth chatter and my legs give way. I hear Missy speaking to me, but her words are drowned out by the white noise roiling inside my head.

"Alex…lie down…it's all right…raise your feet."

I lay powerless on the ground, at the mercy of my thrumming heart.

"Slow, steady breaths," I hear her say. I try to settle my nerves by focusing on whatever surroundings I can identify—the street lights above me, the cool cement on my back.

Missy cradles my head. "It's probably just a panic attack. You'll be fine in a minute. Who is Laura?"

"Who said Laura?"

"You did. Just now."

"No."

"The name Laura has no meaning for you?"

"My daughter."

"Your daughter who died in the accident?"

What does she have to do with anything, and why does this woman keep badgering me? "Long time ago. Three years," I reply weakly.

"Sorry, Alexander, for your loss. Stay with me. How did she die?"

This woman won't let up. I want to tell her to mind her own business, but she has my head in her lap and it feels so soothing, "Drunk driver."

"So senseless. Such a tragedy. I know how long it takes for the heart to heal over something like this. You're lucky in a way to have married, to have known your daughter even for a little while. I was never given that gift. But because Chloe didn't come to term doesn't mean she didn't exist or that I never loved her, does it? Energy doesn't disappear, it just changes form. Hubble doesn't understand that—how sometimes I can see my Chloe the same way you see your Laura."

She's off in her own world and I don't have the strength or the will to engage her.

"I think you being here in Elora is no accident, Alex, and you and I meeting…We have a lot in common. I want to trust you. I'm going to trust you. Are you listening to me?" Through the fog in my head, I hear her say, "I know what happened to the children, where they are, and who took them."

Did I hear her right? I prop myself up on one elbow to try to clear my head, but before she reveals anything more, we're distracted by an argument down the street.

"One more move and I'll punch your lights out."

Missy mutters, "God, haven't we been through enough tonight?"

Without another word, she leaves me to investigate this new disturbance.

"Missy, wait. Who?"

Frustrated and disoriented, I stagger to my feet and stumble after her. When we reach the park, I see that Nathan has Zack pressed up against the pumpkin cart while Zack's friends try to push the big guy off. The kids must have been acting up or something and Nathan with-the-short-fuse overreacted. Constable Clarke is trying to cool down both sides. Now we'll get to the bottom of this. Nothing is going to stop me from telling him what Missy just confided in me.

"Nathan, you back it up right now," I hear the officer warn the big brute.

"Constable? Officer Clarke," I shout.

"Mister Malefant, I thought I told you to stay in your room."

Missy senses what I'm about to say and cuts me off.

"Hubble, Alexander just saw a young girl down on the boardwalk."

"Did you recognize her?" he asks me. "Do you know who she is?"

"Not really," I answer. "She looked to be around seven, eight years old. But…"

Missy interjects again, "Then he saw her again standing on the Tooth." Her eyes warn me against speaking out about the lost children. The balls on that woman! Unfortunately, the constable has taken the bait and latched onto her story like a pit-bull.

"On the Tooth? You're telling me a little girl swam over to the Tooth in the middle of an October night?"

Dammit. If I tell the officer what Missy said, he'll think I'm trying to avoid his questions. And if Missy denies it, who is he going to believe? Her or me?

"I don't know how," I reply, "but she was there like Missy said."

"We both saw her, Hubble."

"Then you must have noticed something about her—hair color, height, what she was wearing." His stare is so intense that I know if I lie he'll see right through me.

"You little asshole!" shouts Big Nathan, who shoves Zack back against the cart.

The two of them begin to scuffle and luckily, the fracas distracts the officer long enough to give Missy and me a moment.

"I know what you're trying to do, Ms. Claridge, but you can't stop me from telling the constable that you have information about…"

"Alexander, look at those three over there,"

she says, pointing at Zack and his two degenerate friends. It takes me a minute, but I see what she's referring to—the way they're dressed. The boys are wearing white tee shirts and blue jeans cut short to show off their white socks and high top sneakers. Sally has her hair in pigtails and wears a red-checkered shirt and poodle skirt. They all could have stepped out of a B movie poster from the 60s. But what does that mean?

"So? Don't change the subject," I argue.

"I'm not changing the subject and I'll tell you everything, I promise. But, where the other children are right now is not as important as protecting them."

"From what?"

Missy nods at the three teens. Is she implying that *they* are the threat?

Zack defends himself to the constable, "I wasn't doing anything illegal unless protecting myself against this Neanderthal is against the law."

Big Nathan wipes some greasy goop out of his thinning hair. "The three of 'em pushed this cart into the square like they owned it, and then they started drawing on these pumpkins. When I asked 'em why, the little snot told me to mind my own bus'ness and then slimed me with some kinda junk from his hair."

"Couldn't find no Brylcream so I used a little Vaseline. You like?" snorts Zack, slicking back his pompadour.

"Zack wasn't doin' nothin' to nobody," clucks his friends. "It's not a crime to move a cart."

"What about defacing public property?" adds Big Nathan.

"We weren't defacing nothing. We were

add-facing," quips Doug. "It's Halloween for Christ sakes."

Now that I have a chance to look over the pumpkins, I see what Big Nathan is croaking about. They've drawn a number of crude faces on them. "This town's had enough Halloween pranks played on it for one night," states the constable, "starting with the costume Zack wore to Missy's house."

The fetus costume. Zack must have known about Missy's miscarriage and worn the thing to taunt her, which is about as low as a person can get. I see Officer Clarke clenching his fists, ready to wail on Zack if given the slightest provocation. He might think Missy is whacko, but clearly, he still has feelings for her. Meanwhile, Zack and his friends glare at Missy with open hostility.

"You had it comin', Bitch," says Zack. "This whole town has it comin'."

If she slapped the kid's face right now, I wouldn't blame her. Clarke reaches for his baton. All hell is about to break loose. Instead, Missy stays Clarke's hand. Her reaction, I think, stemming more from curiosity than revenge. "Had it coming for over fifty years, am I right?" She pulls something out of her pocket.

"What's that?" says Zack.

"A mirror. Thought you might want to fix your hair. It's a little messy and you put so much effort into it."

She hands him a small, round, folded mirror. He opens it to check himself out, but as soon as he does, the image in its face startles him and he turns away. Whatever he saw has left him visibly shaken.

"What is that, some kind of joke?"

Missy smiles and takes the mirror back.

Zack's reaction has confirmed something for her. "So, when the three of you came back from the dump, you called the mayor 'Stubby.'"

"Name of a pickle, ain't it?" cracks Doug.

Zack and his friends chuckle. True, they do seem like a bunch of shiftless punks with no regard for authority, but something tells me they have more on their minds than just stirring up trouble.

Missy makes another odd remark, "Earlier on, the mayor got a visit from the Dunbar Gang, who asked them to help find their killer."

I'm wondering why she would ask Zack. What would he know about it? I'm about to mention that when Missy shoots me a look that tells me to butt out.

"It was a crime that was never solved," says Sally.

"A dirty, rotten crime," adds Doug.

"The murder of thirty-two children who got roasted alive," adds Zack.

Their emphatic replies are not just odd, but telling. If I'm following Missy's reasoning correctly, then we're dealing with something much more complex than three punks raising a little hell on Halloween.

"Hubble, how many pumpkins on this cart? I count twenty-nine," she says. "Twenty-nine and these three makes thirty-two, doesn't it?"

There's a subtle shift in Constable Clarke. The officer follows up on her line of questioning, "Zack, you said you three were out at the dump all night. But you must've known your mom would be worried. Why didn't you call her?"

"With what? It's not like they have a telephone booth out there."

143

I notice Missy drop back to look over the pumpkin cart while the officer presses on.

"Where was your cell?"

Zack looks at his friends and then at Clarke as if the term is foreign to him.

"Your cell phone, Zack?"

"Dunno."

"Doug? Sally? All three of you lost your cell phones?"

Doug and Sally shrug, a gesture that lies somewhere between ignorance and confusion. I hear a funny clicking sound behind me coming from Missy. It's the kind of mindless thing a person does when a piece of a puzzle is found or a lever snaps into place. I'm sensing where Missy is leading Constable Clarke, and it scares me.

Betty marches over from across the street, "I've had enough of this. Is my boy under arrest or not?"

The constable looks from Betty to Zack, and then to Big Nathan.

"Technically speaking, your son assaulted Nathan when he put that guck all over his hair, so I suppose that's up to him. Nathan, you wanna press charges?"

Nathan thinks a moment and shrugs his beefy shoulders. That's enough for the mother hen to send her little chicken hawk and his two friends away before there's any further trouble. "You get yourself home. You're grounded, you hear, Sweetheart?"

Zack and his friends laugh as if this might be the lamest punishment they've ever received. Still, they do what they're told.

I can see that Missy isn't ready to leave

things be. "Betty, have you noticed Zack acting a little strange since he got back?"

"If anyone is strange, Lady, it's you. You're the queen of strange. You keep away from my boy, you twisted bitch, or the Salem witch hunts will seem like a church barbeque, you hear?"

I get the feeling that if it comes to it, both of these women are prepared to throw down, but instead of the claws coming out, Missy smiles and leaves the park. I can't let her go without pressing her, "Missy...?"

"I know, I know, but I need to attend to something first."

"Uh-uh. Nothing is more important than this. Now, you finish what you were going to say about those missing kids, or I'll march right over to Clarke and tell him you're withholding information."

"Listen, no matter what I tell you, you're going to want proof, aren't you? Meet me at my house and I promise I'll have the answer for you and a whole lot more. And don't say anything to anyone until then."

*****

What am I, a fool? Don't tell anyone anything? What if this is a trap? What if she's planning to get me into her house only to do away with me? But then why would she bother to tell me she knows where the kids are in the first place? In my heart, I know that, as weird as that lady is, she wouldn't hurt innocent children, especially after seeing her save Bruce this morning. On the other hand, I saw her make those three teenagers vanish from her street earlier. But even if I allowed for the moment that she might be responsible, it would be quite a stretch to believe that she had the resources to round all of them up by herself and put them in one place without anyone else knowing.

While I ponder this, I hear Rob Vert's voice, "Amanda, take that ridiculous costume off right now. You look like some kind of devil worshipper, for God sakes."

Amanda comes storming into the park dressed in a long, jade-colored robe, black gloves, and white pancake makeup smeared all over her face. "What if I am, Rob? What if that's what it takes to bring our children back?"

"Stop talking nonsense."

"Nonsense? What rational solution have you come up with that's helped to bring our kids back? If all I have to do is accept Satan to have Bruce and Erin come running over that hill, why wouldn't I? And why wouldn't you?"

"I have a better idea. Why don't you and I walk over to church." He tries to lead her by the elbow, but she resists.

"That hall is filled with people. What good has it done any of them? Get down on your knees with me, Rob, right now. Do it for the sake of our children."

"Do what?"

"Pray to the devil!" she orders.

Poor Rob, he's afraid to comply and equally afraid to admit he might be wrong.

"Amanda, please…"

"You pathetic excuse for a man! Get out of my sight!"

Rob's chin drops to his chest, he shakes his head, and walks away like a whipped dog.

Amanda remains glued to the spot,

trembling with self-righteous fury as half the town stares at her. "What're you looking at? If all you want to do is sit around and do nothing, go right ahead. You deserve what you get. Not me!" She closes her eyes and begins to twirl around as if possessed, "Come, Lucifer, Hey, Beelzebub. Here's my offer to you; take this soul for a child or two."

Amanda's chanting is beginning to verge on the macabre. I turn to Constable Clarke to have him do something, anything. "Amanda, stop," He demands. "Amanda!"

She ignores him. Either that or his entreaties are urging her on. Because her twirling morphs into a seductive dance and she begins to rip her blouse with her hands and teeth. "Or if it's something else you want..."

Every man in the vicinity is spellbound. I imagine most have had their own fantasies of this woman at one time or another, and who could blame them?

"Amanda, I'm not going to warn you again."

Amanda drops to her knees and begins moaning and gyrating her hips as if being taken by a lover. The spectacle under this dark October moon is both intoxicating and repulsive at the same time.

One dude steps forward, "You wanna put a little show on for the devil? I'll help ya. No problem."

"And I'm next," says another.

We're on the verge of some serious trouble here. It's the kind of moment when anything could happen. Constable Clarke steps up to the men, daring them to make a move. It's not the officer or the dude who makes the next move, but Betty, who rushes over and covers her sister with a sweater.

"Amanda, stop!"

"Get off me!" she bellows. "It's all right for you. You got your child back."

Betty stubbornly clutches her sister while trying to talk her down, "Remember when we were little? How you were always Daddy's princess? All you had to do was bat an eye and he'd give you anything you wanted? Then when you got older, boys would ask you out every Friday night, you had the pick of the litter at prom? Your children are going to walk over that rise at any minute now because that's the way the world works for you. You're the lucky one, 'Manda, you're the favorite."

Amanda remains rigid, refusing to listen. As much as I dislike the woman, I can't ignore her desperation. When I look past the freaky costume and all her histrionics, I have to admire her determination in doing whatever it takes to get her children back. I can't stand passively by any longer so I step over to her and gently whisper, "Amanda, I think I can help you get your kids back. I know who's behind this."

I don't know exactly, but I'm close. In any case, Amanda is listening. She knows I was privy to her conversation with Ely back at the hotel, so I don't necessarily expect her to trust me. But then our eyes meet and there is a look between us. She senses this is not a ploy, that I want to help her. Betty offers a reassuring smile and all three of us rise to our feet. I ask them to give me a few minutes and I'll meet them at Betty's house. She leads her sister out of the park and I give them a reassuring nod. Amanda gives me a backward glance before she leaves, and I know this time I've done the right thing.

CHAPTER 15

After giving my word to Amanda, I pray my meeting at the witch's house will reveal the whereabouts of the missing children so I can bring back her babies, but life doesn't always play by our rules. You can set a simple course to drive across town. With all the other cars and pedestrians rushing to their own appointments, it's a miracle anybody gets where they're going in one piece. What's that old cliché? "Man plans and God laughs."

As I walk up the street to Missy's house, I notice Ely Shrill having a little discussion with Titus on his porch. The two of them look to be having quite the heart-to-heart. I don't know what they're talking about, but all of a sudden, Titus starts to blubber like a little boy. It's a bit unsettling to see a crusty old man breaking down like that. After a minute, Ely gives him a hug and they say goodbye. Titus closes his door behind him as Ely strolls down to the sidewalk toward me. I'm not sure if he knew I was in the adjacent room when he and Amanda had their confrontation and I really don't want to get into that right now, but I can't ignore him.

"Good evening, Mister Malefant."

"Good evening, Mister Shrill. Is Titus okay?"

"Titus needed to heal some old wounds. I offered him some advice is all."

"You should have given the same advice to Big Nathan. It looked like he could have used it more."

"Perhaps. But there's always some who will listen and some who won't. Which are you?"

"Me?"

"If I could offer you some advice, the issues of the present need to be resolved with those of the past. Until then..."

"You're referring to the deaths of those children fifty years ago? Mister Shrill, I'm in life insurance, I don't expect my clients to know everything about my business, so I try to use plain language. Now, I have no idea who you are or what you do, but maybe if you stopped speaking in riddles, you'd make your point with more clarity and things might get resolved a lot sooner."

I start to walk away, but Ely launches into a story and I'm compelled to stop and listen.

"Alex, I know you want to help. There are several versions of that incident floating around. The way I heard it, back in those days, Fergus was the pumpkin capital of Wellington County. There's not more than six miles between Fergus and Elora, you know. The two shared in the bounty of the land, mutual business interests, and many social activities. But Fergus always won the lion's share at festival time. It was the bigger town. It had more industry, so more people to draw on."

"I know all that. How did the fire start?"

"The people of Elora believed there was some kind of chicanery going on when it came to winning the contests."

"You're saying they were fixed?"

"You can imagine how angry people became after losing year after year. As one version of the story goes, three kids—Brad Dunbar, his girlfriend Doreen Pierce, and Andy Greco—decided to steal

150

the gloomy basement. I remain a few cautious steps behind with the weapon firmly in hand until we're both at the bottom. She snaps on a light bulb above our heads and before me, I see four or five tall shelves, stocked with all kinds of books, opaque bottles and jars. A closer look at these bottles reveals labels, some of which I am familiar. Others sound foreign and vaguely sinister: arsenicum album, stinging nettle, and symphytum cream. There are also mystical symbols on the jars. Missy picks one out for me.

"Genista Tinctoria–recommended for vertigo," she says like a doctor prescribing her medicines. "Pareira Brava relieves urinary symptoms such as black or bloody, thick mucous urine, or when the only way you can pee is to sit on your knees and bear down."

I stare at the bottles, trying to make sense of this woman. "Whoa," is all I can say.

"I believe the word you're looking for, Alexander, is not 'whoa', it's 'Wicca.'"

The term is not foreign to me. I learned about Wicca through a sociology course back in university, I often attended half stoned. "As in devil worship?" I ask.

"As in a religion based on the Earth Mother. Natural remedies—white magic used for good, not bad."

What I remember is that most of the remedies employed by practitioners of Wicca are innocuous enough in small doses, don't do any harm, and generally act as placebos.

"Satan is a Christian concept created to keep the rabble on the straight and narrow. Nothing to do with Wicca."

"I really don't have time for all of this, Missy. I came here because you told me you knew where the children are."

"Not only that, but I know who has them. Me."

"I beg your pardon?"

It takes me a moment to realize that this woman is actually confessing.

"So where are they?"

"On another astral plane, parallel universe, whatever you'd like to call it."

I'm not sure whether to laugh at her or throw a net over her. In any case, I tighten my grip on the frying pan.

"You and Ely must be drinking the same Kool-Aid. But I'll bite, why?"

"To protect them from a larger menace."

She extracts something from her purse— three small glass balls strung together on a cord.

"What is that?

As Missy ties the balls to a beam above us she explains her reason for "removing" the children from town in the first place by first recounting the supernatural phenomena we were witness to—the episode where young Bruce was almost drowned by a spirit hiding inside the apple barrel, the crow attack, and the apparitions reaching out to her through Big Nathan's store window.

In her words, those were attempts by otherworldly entities trying to breach our physical plane. That's why when she first suspected it, she suggested the town postpone the Halloween dance. Her only concern was to keep the children of Elora out of harm's way until she could figure out a way to stop the "invasion."

I remind her of the three teens who egged her house, the ones I saw her make disappear. This, she confesses, was a mistake she committed out of rage against Zack's insensitive choice of costume. She was so upset by Zack's taunting of her unborn child, that she banished him and his two friends to the garbage dump to cool their heels for a while.

"That explains why they were wearing shoes."

"I left all the other children's shoes in the tree to show the parents that they were coming back, to give them hope. I guess I didn't do a very good job of it."

"So when those three came back over the ridge, that wasn't Ely's doing?" I ask.

"Please! That charlatan? He did nothing but take the credit."

"And when Mary Novak told us about her husband being questioned by three spirits…"

"…the possession had already taken place. That's why Zack and his friends weren't spirited away with the others. The souls of our three and the spirits of those three had already fused."

"Which is how they knew the mayor's nickname, Stubby?"

Missy nods, "You asked me what Zack saw in the scrying mirror that frightened him so much."

"You said his true self."

"What he saw was the ghost that possessed him, what was and is inhabiting him. Earlier at the park, you'll remember there were twenty-nine pumpkins on the cart. Zack and his friends make it thirty-two. There are others are out there waiting right now to be summoned. If they succeed…"

She weaves a good story, I'll give her that. I

think that she truly believes she's the town's shaman and chief defender. That's what scares me. I've read accounts about mothers with postpartum depression who kill their children to save them from what they believe is a worse fate—demons, the devil coming after them. I wonder if that's what I'm dealing with here. That the children are missing there is no doubt. Whether she killed them or stashed them somewhere in a barn or a cave to save them is the question. Right now I'm the only person she trusts, so I need to play along even though everything in me tells me to run the other way.

"But with all you've said, you have yet to show me proof..."

She points to three glass balls hanging above our heads. "They're called witch balls, glass orbs used by many cultures and faiths around the world to ward off evil. Look closely."

They look like tiny fishbowls with even tinier fish swimming inside...until I realize those aren't fish.

"Your eyes do not deceive you, Alexander. What you see is real."

But my eyes *do* deceive me. They must. Maybe she hypnotized me or dabbed a topical drug onto my skin from one of those sinister-looking bottles when I wasn't looking.

"Is that Zack inside there?"

"And Sally and Doug, along with the spirits who have possessed them." She waves at the teenagers imprisoned in each ball. Their faces are clearly visible, and their mouths are working feverishly but silently, begging to be freed.

"I put them there until I could find a way to deal with them."

I don't know what to say. I was somewhat prepared for Missy to lead me to a place filled with dead bodies. But this? I want to say I'm relieved, but now I have to face the fact that everything she said might actually be true. "I don't know how you did this, Missy, but you have to let them go right now. It's...it's inhumane."

"You haven't been listening, Alex. The spirits from the past have possessed our children so that they could come back and find their killer. Not only did I fail to stop this from happening, but I helped enable it. It must be as clear to you as it is to me that we're never going to solve our problem until we solve theirs. And that means we need to learn as much as we can about the fire of '64. We haven't got much time. Like I said, more are trying to find their way over as we speak. And then who knows what could happen?"

"I...I don't know what to say."

"Say, 'I believe you, Missy, and I'll help you.' You wanted proof, goddammit! Here it is. How long are you going to keep denying what's right in front of your eyes?" She flicks one of the witch balls and the horror on the faces of those children, or ghosts, or whatever they are, freezes my blood.

"If not them, think about yourself, Alexander. Until we act, you'll never be free of this town and everyone in it—including that little ghost-girl who keeps popping up to haunt you."

As crazy as she sounds, there is an undeniable ring of truth to it.

"Let's say I take your word for the moment. What do you suggest?"

She smiles as if I'd showered her with a

thousand kisses. "We need to speak to Percy, Titus, any of the old farts who were around in those days. We need to find out what really happened. Come on. We're wasting time."

She places the orbs back in her pouch and pushes me toward the stairs. "The more I think about it, the more I'm convinced taking the children was the right thing to do because ultimately, they'll lead us to the truth. That's what children do, you know, they show you the truth." Missy speaks with such fervor that I'm almost convinced. I watch her skip up the steps with the energy of a child herself. When she reaches the top, she opens the door and I hear a thud! Next thing I know, a foot lashes out, kicking me in the stomach, sending me backward. There's a sharp crack on the back of my head, and I'm swallowed by the void.

CHAPTER 16

Head throbs...back hurts...brain is lit up like a Roman Candle...body is wracked with pain. *What do you do?*

Swimming slowly to consciousness, I lie in the pitch black, worrying whether I'll ever get up again. I'm cognizant enough to try to do some kind of physical assessment. I start with my toes, which triggers a sharp pain in my ankle. Maybe a twist there. I move higher up my legs. Nothing feels broken. Hips are bruised, ribs hurt when I breathe, and it's cold against my cheekbone. I'm lying face down on concrete. *What do you do with a...*

I force myself from elbow to knee, at which point, I puke. The vomiting settles my stomach, but the collateral effect is like a whack to the head. When I touch it, it feels wet...I'm bleeding. I reach for something to help me to my feet and find a rack of shelves. I'm in Missy's basement, been kicked down the stairs. The last thing I remember before I blacked out is a voice, *What do you do with a...*a loop that keeps running through my head. A woman's voice. Not Missy's.

I swat the air above me until I catch a string of metal beads with my fingers. When I switch on the light bulb above, I find my hands bloody from the gash on my head. Bruised and battered, I work my way up the stairs a step at a time, which confirms at least that nothing is broken. Can I make it all the way up? Damn phrase repeats with every step, *What do you do...what do you do with a...*

When I reach the top, I turn the knob and nervously open the door. No more surprises, please.

The moon shining through the faded drapes offers just enough light to help me navigate around the shabby furniture. The place is empty. No sounds, no signs of Missy. Missy...*What do you do with a witch?* That's it—the phrase spoken by the woman who drop-kicked me down the stairs.

I stumble out the front door to get some fresh air, but it's still oppressively thick outside. If this isn't the hottest Halloween on record...and then it hits me that it's still hot and it's still night time. Nothing has changed. How long has it been since sundown? Ten, twelve hours at least, although my watch still reads 7:00. More confused than ever, I stumble down the street toward the town center to get some medical attention. I pass a few bewildered couples and ask for help, but nobody pays me any mind. Why should they? They have their own troubles. I keep wandering until I notice something new in the air, the smell of decay.

I follow my nose to the park, worried what that smell is going to reveal. Then I see the source of the foul odor—the food sitting on the tables. Rot has set in. Insects have laid their eggs. All the pies, vegetables, and fruit have become infested with bugs, their larvae squirming in the sticky goo. This whole town is rotting from the inside. Residents wander through the area, holding their noses against the stench, but nobody makes a move to clean the mess or pay me any mind. Nobody except Ely Shrill who leans on the pumpkin cart. With a nod, he invites me over.

"Got a nice ripe cut on your head, Mister Malefant. Looks like you've had quite a time."

"Quite," is all I can manage. I don't want to say anything more. I don't trust the guy.

He reaches over and grabs a nearby folding chair, gesturing for me to sit. He steps away and after a few seconds, returns with a damp cloth, which he places on my head. I have to admit, it feels good. As he cleans my wound, I look over the decaying food. "It just goes from bad to worse around here."

"Did you expect things to get better all by themselves?"

"No. But, what brought you here, Mister Shrill?"

"Same as you."

"Doubt it. I'm in insurance."

"Oh, I know what you do. Everybody in Elora knows what you do. And they also know that when you couldn't do any business you looked for the quickest way out. Now you're surprised that nobody offers you any help."

"You make it sound like I don't care about those missing kids. Well, you and everybody else in this God-forsaken town are wrong. I just came from Missy's house to try to get to the bottom of this and got kicked down a flight of stairs for my trouble."

"All of which has brought you here."

"To the park to stare at a bunch of rotting fruit," I reply sarcastically.

"And what else, Alexander?"

Ely steps aside to allow me a better look at the pumpkin cart. The last time I saw the melons, Zack and his friends had drawn crude faces on them. Now it looks as though those sketches have morphed into more detailed images of children.

"Mister Shrill, I really don't know what you're trying to say–as usual. My head is splitting, my ribs are aching, and to tell you the truth, I'm sick and tired of all your riddles. I am sick of you."

"And yet I was the only one who brought you a wet cloth for your blood-soaked head." He's got a point. "Humor me, Mister Malefant. Centuries ago, people believed in a hundred gods—one for war, one for love, another for revenge. As time went by, they came to believe in a single God with a hundred different names–Jesus, Yaweh, Allah. A half century ago, someone declared God was dead altogether and science was the new religion. So, of all of them, who is right?"

"I'm not a philosopher. Is there a point to this gibberish?"

"Let's try another tack. You're in insurance. Some of your clients believe in burial, others in cremation. Which of them is right?"

"I tell people it's their choice."

"Wise answer. Now, Missy believes in the Earth Mother, Rob Vert believes in God, Deputy Art believes in the Multiverse. Who is right and who is wrong?" I cannot answer that. "Could God, and Mother Earth, and the Multiverse all exist alongside each other? Is it possible that there's more than one interpretation to life?"

"Please. If you're comparing Missy's Wiccan beliefs to scientific theory, you're as crazy as she is."

"According to quantum physics, an object can be in two places at one time. According to Missy and myself, the children are both here and on a different astral plane."

"Quantum theory has been proved."

"To those who *believe* in science. God has also been proved to those who believe in religion. Don't you see that we're all talking about the same

162

thing, just using different terms?"

"Again, I am not a…who the hell are you, Mister Shrill?"

"A friend here to help you find Missy, find that little girl you've been chasing, find your own peace of mind. But to do that, you need to open your eyes." A black crow lands on his shoulder. He pets it and walks away.

This whole town has gone bat-shit. My encounter with Ely has only left me with more questions, one of which is *how did he know about the little girl*? I never mentioned her to him.

A woman screams and drops to the ground in a dead faint. Others gasp. One of the pumpkins on the cart moves as if something is trying to emerge from it. Bulges appear through the thick skin until a crack materializes, and fleshy fingers claw out. More pumpkins quiver and tremble until shards of peel burst and splatter over everyone. Arms and legs reach out of the pulpy goo, followed by torsos that wriggle after them. People are being birthed in all their fleshy gore! Their faces look like the faces that were etched into those pumpkins. More and more melons burst until, after a minute or so, the eruptions subside and there are dozens of boys and girls. There's no logical explanation for this: no reference point, no scientific basis. *Who are they, where did they come from, what do they want?* The only explanation that comes to mind is Missy's theory that these are the children she warned us about, the ones who died in the fire fifty years ago and have come back to find their killer. *Missy, where the hell are you?*

CHAPTER 17

I leave the park and jog up the street while I rack my brain for a clue as to where to find that woman. She's not at home, she's not at the park, and no one I've spoken to has seen her. So, who haven't I spoken to? Who haven't I seen?

I find my car on the bridge where I left it and drive over to Amanda's house. The lights are off and no one answers when I knock. I sniff around the side doors and windows to see if anyone might be inside, but the place looks vacant. What the hell, this is an emergency. I smash the patio window, enter, and wait for a reaction. That's one way to find out if anyone is home. I've been in this house before so it's not hard to navigate from room to room. My immediate fear is over what I might find, or what I don't find. There's also another niggling concern—getting caught for breaking and entering. No question I'd lose my insurance license, but I suppose in the scheme of things, that's pretty minor. I go room to room on every floor. There's no one here. I leave the Vert residence and head for my next stop—Betty's. No one home there either.

The only other person I know who might have a clue is Titus. When I get to his house, I hear music. It's sweet and innocent, the kind of tune that a child might enjoy. I sneak up to the front window to peek inside. Titus is sitting in a chair, smiling and laughing. There are two others inside, but I can only see their shadows as they flit around the room. I've never seen the old postman in a good mood and, for some reason, it feels like one of those what's-wrong-with-this-picture kinds of moments. Panic engulfs me. I run around to the front and knock on the door. The music stops and Titus opens up.

"Hey, Titus, I'm, uh, looking for Missy."

"Not here."

"Well the thing is, I'm worried about her. Maybe I could ask your friends inside?"

I try to force my way in, but Titus's foot is wedged in behind the door and I can't budge it.

"Ain't no one else here."

"You're lying. I heard music. I saw people dancing."

"You saw nothing, you heard nothing, I have to tell you nothing 'cept Missy ain't here and never was. Now get out."

With that, the old coot shuts the door on me. A minute later, the music starts up again. I peek through the window, but all I can see is Titus sitting in a chair with his flask, smiling. I turn away feeling hopeless and stupid. Mysteries pop up in every corner of the town, Missy is, well, missing, and I'm out of options. And then I see her. Not Missy—the little girl I'd been chasing, standing down the block.

I can either take another run at her or try a different approach. "Please, I won't hurt you."

She doesn't run this time, but she doesn't answer either. I take a step forward and she takes one back.

"Would you like to play a game? How about if I guess your name you help me find someone I'm looking for. I bet your name is...Chloe? Am I right? Chloe, I'm worried about your mother, that if we don't find her soon it might be bad for her. Will you help me?"

She nods and beckons me to follow. If you had told me twenty-four hours ago I'd be chasing some prepubescent ghost into the woods to find her mother, the witch...

Chloe leads me down the block to a place named "HOFFER PARK" which leads to another wooded area they call "VICTORIA PARK". This is the last place I'd want to venture at night, but it *is* an ideal place to hide someone. It's also a great place for a murder. I can see several hiking paths leading into the forest. The one Chloe leads me along is covered with white pebbles and is shrouded by trees with large, overhanging branches. They remind me of mourners at a funeral. I ask her to slow down, but she ignores me, and I know that if I don't keep up, I will have lost my only chance at finding Missy.

A short distance along, we reach a five-foot high fence that stretches for hundreds of feet in both directions. It must have been built to prevent hikers and idiots like me from falling into the gorge that drops steeply off on the other side. The child turns right, and after a few hundred feet we end up at a concrete platform overlooking the gorge. They call it "LOVER'S LEAP". There's a plaque, somebody's idea of a marketing tool that tells the story of an Indian princess who took her life after her lover died in battle. Please tell me Missy didn't take a header from here. Apparently not, because the child runs away again.

I meet up with her several hundred feet ahead by a steep staircase that leads down into the rocky gorge. As soon as she sees me, she descends, and all I can do is pray that I don't break my neck as I try to keep up. Thankfully, there's a metal railing to grab onto because these granite block steps could be treacherous, day or night. When we arrive at the forest floor, it feels as if I've entered a primordial forest. We are surrounded by gnarled trees and huge boulders. The moonlight shining down on the cliff walls illuminate caves that could be portals to distant, magical lands. Behind me I hear the water thundering over the falls, and in front of me are the sounds of a thousand night creatures. Chloe is already at the river's edge where the flow is fast and dangerous. She treads easily over the slick stones that dot the bank, but my Tom McCanns aren't made for hiking. I call out for her to slow down, but she ignores me as usual. Suddenly, she veers off into a break and I'm left alone.

Damn! If someone had intended to lose me in the wilderness, I couldn't have made it any easier for them. Eventually, I reach the turn she made and spot a narrow path leading into the woods. Twenty feet ahead or so are voices. I've developed enough smarts by now to know this could be an ambush, so I crouch down and proceed as quietly as I can. Look at me, Secret Insurance Agent Man crawling through the underbrush on my hands and knees.

"I did some reading up on witches," says one nasty voice. "I learned that burning them is a cleansing ritual. Gets rid of evil."

"Only if the witch is evil." That's Missy, responding.

"As if any witch is good," replies a third voice. "Especially one who kidnaps innocent children and holds them prisoner in such monstrous traps."

Now I recognize the two other voices— Betty and Amanda. All three are in a clearing ten feet away and what I see ties my stomach in knots.

Missy is bound to a tree, ankle deep in kindling and branches. Betty holds the three glass orbs in front of her, while Amanda stands off to the side with a torch at the ready.

What do you do with a witch? Burn her.

This is my fault. I was the one who told the sisters I knew who was behind this. They must have followed me to Missy's house and laid in wait. I crawl toward them, careful not to break a branch or give myself away. These women managed to knock me out and kidnap Missy, so I'm not going to underestimate them a second time.

"Those aren't your children," replies Missy.

"Liar," Betty says. "I can see Zack trapped in this devil-glass plain as day. You free him and his friends right now, and then you free Amanda's kids from wherever you're holding them. Or else."

Amanda lowers the torch to the kindling. The forest goes eerily quiet as if all the night creatures anticipate some heinous crime about to be committed. By the look on the women's faces, it's plain that they're not only capable of making good on their threat, but are so far gone that they might even relish it. Still, Missy refuses to cave. Amanda hisses like a snake and drops the torch onto the tinder by Missy's feet, setting it aflame. "We're serious, Witch."

"So are they," replies Missy.

An animal growls several yards to the left of me. The sisters whip around to find four sets of feral eyes staring at them from the underbrush. Wolves. A crow swoops down from a tree and grazes Betty's head, causing her to drop the three orbs onto the kindling.

"Betty, keep the glass away from the fire!"

warns Missy as she tries to kick the branches at her feet.

The wolves creep threateningly toward the women who are frozen to the spot. As the animals advance, I realize the ladies are not the only ones in danger. Those wolves have also noticed me. Should I run? Should I freeze? Does playing dead go for wolves, or bears, or for forest creatures in general? These beasts are so close now that I can smell the dander on their fur and see the menace in their eyes. *I am not the enemy, I am not the enemy.* They stop to sniff me and then, mercifully, they, slink past.

Another crow swoops down on Amanda and makes her stumble onto the fire, scorching her feet. She shrieks and kicks the wood, which only serves to fan the flames. While Amanda is distracted, the alpha wolf heads for Missy, and the other three surround the sisters.

Missy stares her wolf in the eye. I'm not sure if this is a survival tactic or she's communicating with it. Meanwhile, the flames have grown in intensity and her skirt catches fire. I don't know how she can stand the heat, but she seems more concerned with the orbs than herself. I can't let this happen, I can't let her burn. I get to my feet and charge awkwardly through the bush. "Missy!"

"Alex, stay where you are!"

Too late. By the time she's warned me, I've skidded into the middle of the clearing and made myself a target.

"A murder of wolves?" I ask.

"A pack of wolves," Missy answers.

"Thanks for the clarification. And your skirt is on fire."

Ignoring my warning, she points to the glass

orbs by her feet, "Alex, if those orbs burn, the children inside will perish."

I take a step toward them, and one of the wolves bares his fangs. "Can you call them off?"

"Don't know if they'll listen. Fire makes 'em crazy."

The flames are starting to lick Missy's torso now. She's about to be burned alive, yet she's more concerned about the damn orbs.

I take a step toward her and one of the wolves takes one toward me. I'm not going to get by this animal, and I'm not going to out-wrestle it either. I remember one of the first things I learned in sales was that when I entered a client's house, make friends with the family pet. I smile and offer my closed hand to prevent any nipping. Good puppy.

The animal takes a step closer to sniff my trembling hand.

"Alex, the orbs," she urges as the flames hiss around her.

Carefully, I side-step the wolf to show I am not a direct threat, and inch toward the fire. When I'm close enough, I kick the orbs away from the flames. With my hand still out to the beast, I begin to kick the wood away from Missy's feet. Her clothing has lit her up like a torch. I don't know how she can stand there without screaming. I grab her skirt and pull. It comes off in flaming shreds but at least the immediate threat is gone.

"Trenches," Missy orders.

I look around to find a hefty branch lying about a foot away and pick it up. The wolves growl, but only because they're as afraid of the fire as I am. Hopefully they understand I'm trying to help. I jab the earth to loosen the dirt, then kick it onto the flames. All the while, I'm smiling like an idiot and chanting, "Good puppy, nice puppy." I must be the biggest dork in the forest.

Amanda and Betty follow my lead and help dig trenches to keep the fire from spreading. The three wolves allow us to continue while the fourth goes behind Missy and gnaws through her ropes. After a few interminable minutes, we've extinguished the flames. Covered in soot and sweat, I look up to find all four wolves at Missy's side. I cringe at the sight of the blisters running along her limbs. I wouldn't blame her if she sic'd the wolves on the women. Instead, she extends her burnt hands to the alpha wolf and it licks her. The other wolves join in, covering her legs and hands with saliva. A moment later, they leave the clearing.

"You two all right?" I ask the Trout sisters. "And are you crazy?"

Betty remains stubbornly adamant. "She's a witch and she stole our children! I heard her say so with my own two ears. If no one else was going to do something, we had to."

Amanda props up her sister, "My children are missing and nobody's doing shit about it!"

"Even so, you can't burn people at the stake. This isn't the Inquisition."

"What would you do, if it was your child?"

"I don't know, but not this."

While Amanda and I argue, Betty remembers the orbs and lunges. Before she can scoop them up, a crow swoops down and carries them to a branch high over our heads.

"My baby!" Betty cries.

"Now what?" asks Amanda.

"Wait here, all of you," I order.

It's not enough that I have to trek down into a deep, dark gorge, trip along a dicey riverbank, and face four angry wolves. Now I have to climb a tree and face-off with a rogue crow. I begin my climb, taking one branch at a time, careful not to scare away the bird as it stares me down. When I'm about a foot away, I gingerly reach up to grab the hanging orbs. That's when I notice a strange light at the top of the escarpment hanging like a canopy over the town. At the same moment, the demon bird chooses to peck my hand and loosen my grip. Free-falling through a thousand needle-like branches, I land with a bone-crushing thunk. Middle management, pencil-pushing, fast-food bred bodies like mine were not built for this kind of punishment. Through the pain and the dirt and tears, I see the women hover over me. At first, I think they're thanking me for risking my life. Then I realize they're lambasting me for letting the crow get away with their precious children. Can I not get a break?

CHAPTER 18

Missy checks me for any broken bones or twisted joints. Thankfully, I'm relatively unscathed. While she's doing that, I realize she has no skirt on, just a blouse that falls over her naked limbs. I remember those wretched heat blisters and although I'm embarrassed to look, I have to sneak a peek. Amazingly, her calluses and burns have faded. She smiles. "Appears those remedies in my basement weren't placebos after all. Those and the wolf saliva balm."

After we've assessed each other, I fill Missy and the others in on the spirits that were "birthed" out of the pumpkins back in the town square.

"We need to get back there now," warns Missy with an ominous tone.

"What about our babies?" says Betty.

The Trout sisters look utterly crushed. Amanda's shoulders droop with despair.

I turn to Missy. "As annoying and obnoxious as these two are, you need to tell them what you told me. You owe them that much."

Missy explains to Amanda and Betty what she did, confirming their suspicions, but more importantly, her reason for taking the children—to keep them out of harm's way.

"So bring them back!" demands Amanda.

"Not until we've dealt with these others who have invaded Elora. Until then, our children are still in danger. And after what Alex just told us, it's not only the children who are in jeopardy. It's the whole damn town."

After a little more back-and-forth, we agree

to put our differences aside and head back to the village. The four of us trudge along the riverbank and backup the staircase in silence. Along the way, the Trout sisters strip off some of their garments to help Missy cover herself. When she and I are alone for a minute, she says, "Alex, thanks for coming after me. I really didn't expect that. But I gotta ask, how did you know where to find me?"

"Your daughter, Chloe. She's the little girl I've been seeing all over town. She led me to you."

Missy smiles, "Thanks for believing."

A silly thought comes to mind. "It's funny. I talk to people all the time about their last wishes, cremation, and such. It's just that I don't generally discuss it with them *after* the fact."

"Shows you there's a first for everything. All kidding aside, Alex, it takes courage to step out of your comfort zone. Most people wouldn't. But then again, you switched careers in midlife, and that says something."

"Oh, I didn't change careers so much as got shifted around by the company is all. After my daughter died, I was no good around the office. I'd been with the firm for over twenty years, so rather than let me go, they put me on the road."

"Do you like it? The road?"

"I love seeing the countryside and the people, and I love bringing them..."

"... 'peace of mind.' I know. But with all you've been through, did it never occur to you that maybe this journey is meant to bring *you* peace of mind?"

When we reach the top of the escarpment, we all notice an acrid smell. Nothing is said but it confirms my fears about that portentous glow over the town I saw earlier. We hurry back through Hoffer Park toward the town center. When we get there, the place is vacant. No residents, no ghost children. All we see is the scorched pumpkin cart and burnt husks that lie cracked and smoldering everywhere.

"You were right, Betty," says Missy. "Fire is a cleansing ritual, but not always for the right reasons."

We turn toward Metcalfe Street to see black plumes of smoke and bright orange flames licking the night sky. The business section is in utter chaos. Cars are on fire, windows are shattered, and store merchandise is strewn all over the pavement. The ominous threat that emerged from those pumpkins has been unleashed all over whole town. The entities I saw earlier are on a rampage.

"Oh my God!" says Missy.

"This is what you were afraid of, isn't it?" I ask her.

"What I'm really afraid of is that this is only the beginning."

Missy warned us that these ghost children would seek revenge if we didn't help them find their murderers, and now they're making good on their promise—driving cars into lamp posts, destroying everything in sight.

Terrified residents run for cover and cower in every shadow. Constable Clarke races from one crisis to another. Deputy Art tries to collar one of the hooligans, "Come here ya little snot…"

But the deputy is out of his league. The pint-sized apparitions outrun and outmaneuver him at every turn. No one can catch them, let alone stop them. All anyone can do is stay out of their way.

Then something flies overhead, and everyone stops in their tracks.

"What's that?" asks Betty.

It's the crow from the forest and it has the orbs in its claws. I watch it land on the green church steeple and drop the string of glass balls. They roll down the slanted roof to the eaves trough and continue toward the vertical down spill. The orbs drop down the tube, out the spout, and smash on the ground. Betty and Amanda issue an anguished cry, convinced that the souls trapped inside have perished. But the act actually frees them and restores them to their former selves.

"Zack! Come to Momma, Baby," shouts Betty.

All she gets is a sarcastic laugh.

"I told you that isn't Zack," says Missy.

The adolescent horde squeals with delight upon seeing their comrades restored, and they continue to destroy the town with renewed vigor. At this rate, the town will be decimated within the hour.

"Pity."

There's no mistaking that voice. It belongs to Ely Shrill. The gaunt albino steps out of a bakery munching a Danish sweet. With a self-satisfied smile, he stands there like a proud papa admiring his brood. Clarke charges him and shoves him against a wall.

"Make 'em stop!"

"As I said, I am only a facilitator."

"Then facilitate them to stop."

"I can't, Officer, but *you* can."

"You know what, Mister Shrill, I've had enough of your crap," shouts the officer.

Hubble pulls a pair of handcuffs from his belt, slaps them on Ely's wrists, and secures him to a lamp post. "We don't know who killed those kids, and right now, I don't care. What I do care about is my town and the people in it, including Missy Claridge. So you're not going anywhere until..."

"...Hubble?" shouts Missy. She leaves our bedraggled group and races into Hubble's arms. "Nice to know you were worried about me," she purrs.

"I was never worried about you. I was worried what you'd do to whoever tried to hurt you."

Constable Clarke looks over Missy's shoulder and nods a "thank you" to me for having found his girlfriend. He turns to Betty and Amanda who stand there looking guilty as sin. "Where were you all? What happened?"

"She's the one who took our kids," replies Amanda. "She admitted it."

Constable Clarke looks at Missy who doesn't deny Amanda's claim. Before she can explain further, we're distracted by Deputy Art who has cornered a few of the hooligans. "Freeze. I got 'em, Hubble."

It looks like the deputy is the one about to be cornered when a car barrels down the street directly at him. Trembling with fear, he fumbles with the safety clip on his holster. It's obvious that he's never had to use his firearm. He finally frees his gun and shoots, blowing out the windshield. The car veers to the right and crashes into a light standard.

No one could have survived that. No human, anyway. Amazingly, a fifteen-year-old "boy" pulls himself out of the rubble and marches over to Art, handing him a fistful of bullets. Before Art can say, "what the hell?" a dozen crows dive-bomb him. The deputy shoots at the birds, but it's no use, there are too many. They peck at the poor bastard's hands and face until he drops to his knees. Clarke fires off a couple of shots to scare the pests away while Missy and I carry Art to safety. The random shots don't do much to stop the birds until the quick-thinking constable points his weapon at Ely's head.

"Why do I have the feeling that you can make them stop?" he asks the albino.

Ely closes his eyes as if in prayer, and the birds fly off as suddenly as they appeared. The ghost-children cease their attack and retreat to a neutral position up the street. It looks like we have a reprieve. Amanda rushes over to Art who sits on the ground, weeping. "Arthur, are you all right?"

"My eyes...I can't see!"

Amanda tears a swatch from her skirt and dabs the blood on his face. It's an act of comfort, but there's something more to it. As she cradles his head to her breast, it becomes clear as to why Betty is so jealous of her sister. It's also clear why Art was so ashamed of some of the things he's been up to.

None of this is lost on the constable, but he's got more on his mind at the moment than a randy deputy. "Keep applying pressure to the wounds. Somebody, we need medical supplies."

Betty is off like a shot across the street to the drug store. Furiously she shakes the locked doors until someone points out that the windows have already been blown out. Embarrassed, she steps through the frame. Under different circumstances it would make for a comical moment. A minute later, returns with a handful of gauze, tape, and ointments. Together, the sisters apply the remedies to Art's eyes and hands. The two work hand in hand. No words are spoken or need to be. As miserable as the deputy might be feeling right now, my sympathy goes to Rob. For my money, he's the one who's been wronged.

With the situation stable, Clarke levels his steely gaze at the Trout sisters. "Now, I want to know what happened between you and Missy out there, and I want the truth."

"It was all a big mistake," replies Missy, as if to minimize the incident.

But Clarke isn't going to be sloughed off and turns to me for an explanation, "Alexander?"

Why me all the time? If I tell the officer that these two had Missy tied to a tree and were burning her at the stake, he's liable to skin them alive. So I launch into a story about seeing a young girl who led me to the three women at the bottom of the gorge and then being threatened by a pack of wolves. After I've detailed the account with the glass orbs and the thieving crow, whatever the women were doing down there in the first place becomes inconsequential. Then I wonder aloud about who or what was trying to get us out of the way so that the ghost children could invade the town. By the time I've finished my tale, I'm almost proud of myself.

Missy picks it up from there and concludes with, "Hubble, we're all to blame. We've ignored the warning signs and wasted too much time. What we need to do right now is deal with those spirits."

I know what she's thinking. Ely Shrill is the only person who has any sway with these vicious apparitions, but when Clarke and the rest of us turn to the lamppost where he was secured, he's gone. In his place is a large, white bird that slips out of its shackles, flaps his wings, and takes flight. What are we to believe: that one took the place of the other, or that one and the other are the same? Is that mythological story about the crow to be taken literally?

None of us knows when the next attack will occur, only that it will. Taking advantage of the pause in hostilities, Constable Clarke moves us all down the street, away from the carnage. Betty and Amanda escort the near-blind Art as tears of pain and self-pity rain down his cheeks. I look around at our rag-tag group and oddly, it brings to mind the reason I took up a career in insurance.

"You know, I sit with people every day and talk to them about protecting their families and how they want to be remembered. They tell me that they've thought about it for months, sometimes years, but they never get around to it. Until a family member dies. Then, after we've put something in place, they feel better, but when it comes to this town, it feels like nothing was put in place. Nobody thought to make peace with the past or consider the future."

"No peace of mind for any of us, Mister Malefant," says Amanda.

Whatever I said must have resonated with Missy because she suddenly grabs Constable Clarke by the sleeve and turns to him. "Hubble, after I lost the baby, I was very angry at the world. I ranted and raved and I went a little crazy, I know—I pushed everybody away, including you. I'm sorry for that. Sometimes, I'd go into the woods and scream like a banshee. It felt good. It felt so good that I started going out there a lot. The more I did, the more that wilderness became a haven for me. I needed to believe that Chloe's soul and my soul were somehow connected, that the experience happened and wasn't something to bury and forget. Nobody here would believe me. But out there it could be real. *She* could be real. And that's when she came back to me."

No one says a word or denies the validity of her claim, not even Constable Clarke. With children being birthed out of pumpkins, the town overrun by ghosts, and these random crow attacks, how much stranger is it to believe that the ghost of one's daughter has returned? Or even existed? After a long silence, he replies, "I'm sorry I gave you the cold shoulder and ignored you at times. It's amazing how clever we can be at blocking out the things we don't want to deal with. I think you're right, Malefant. Everything we're going through now is a way of making us face what we've denied for years."

"Finally!" Missy shouts.

We continue walking past burnt-out restaurants, nail spas, and abandoned cars. The town looks like a war zone, its heart and soul gutted from the inside.

"They really went to town on the town, didn't they?" says the constable. "So, Missy, how would we go about setting things straight?"

For the first time, Missy looks stumped. I think she was expecting that when the time came, the answer would magically appear like a unicorn on the horizon or perhaps Mother Earth would come charging up in a chariot and hand her a golden apple. *Now I'm inventing my own myths.*

"What do you want?" she shouts to the heavens. "We're ready. Tell us." Then, she runs over to the park. We follow her to the statue of The Tall Guy. Maybe there's an envelope in his hands with the answer tucked inside. Personally, I think that if that dude could, he'd pull his long lanky legs out of the concrete and walk away in disgust. In any case, there's no envelope, no answer, no remedy.

Amanda drops to her knees in total despair. "I can't anymore."

Who can argue with her? Everything we do only seems to make things worse. Across the street, the church door opens. Mayor Novak, his wife Mary, Titus, Rob Vert, and a few other bedraggled souls emerge. Rob spots his wife hunched over the base of the statue and hurries over. If this was a fairy tale ending, they'd kiss and everyone would break into a rousing rendition of "All You Need Is Love." But, that's not happening.

"Amanda, Honey?"

Amanda ignores her husband, either ashamed of herself or beyond consolation altogether. That's when I notice something. Virtually everyone in this town looks crushed. Everyone except Titus who is standing around with a strange look of...anticipation on his face. Missy and the constable are having a moment and I don't want to disturb them. So I turn to the only other person who might shed a little light. "Nathan, you know Titus pretty well."

"I've had nothing to do with him for years."

"Sure, but when I passed his house earlier, I noticed there were lights on and music playing, like a party going on. And now, look at him."

"What can I say? Titus is a strange dude. That fire years back? He lost his daughter to it. A year later, his wife died. He goes in and out. We all got our own ways of coping."

Nathan is right; we all have our coping mechanisms. I guess Titus needs to pretend.

In the past few hours, the people of this town have lost their children, their homes, and have been cut off from the rest of the world. Businesses and buildings along their proud little main street are in ruins, and the people who ran them have been terrorized. And yet, I feel the worst is yet to come.

Right on cue, one of the residents senses something down the block, and like a herd of frightened deer, we're all alerted to it. There they are—Ely and his "children" lined up across the street like an army of the damned waiting to attack. Missy was right all along, we should have dealt with them first. Now that we need her, where is she? Constable Clarke takes a few tentative steps toward the intruders, but there's no confidence in his walk. The rest of us follow in loose formation, resigned to the fact that this will all end soon, one way or the other. When we get within distance, the constable reaches for his gun—the desperate move of a man bankrupt of choices.

"Is that really the best option, Constable?" asks Ely with a smirk.

"It's all you've left me."

"Have you ever watched a monkey try to open a can of beans? It'll smash it and stomp on it and throw it against a tree, but the can will not open. Why? Because the monkey doesn't have a can opener. Nor would he know what to do with it if he had one. You've prayed to God, you've prayed to the devil, and you've blamed each other."

"So you're saying we're using the wrong tools for the job. We're going at this the wrong way?"

While Ely and the constable are parlaying, I notice Titus march up to the ghost-like figures. He opens his hand to show them something.

Ely continues, "Have been for as long as anyone can remember. Why do you think it's come to this? You can only run from your ghosts for so long."

The phantoms acknowledge whatever Titus has shown them. The line divides in two and reveals two other figures that come forward—a black woman and her young daughter. It doesn't take much to figure out who they are. They reach out to Titus and wrap him up in their embrace. Tears of joy stream down the old man's cheeks.

"I'll be," gasps Nathan.

Titus's wife and daughter take him by the hand and lead him back through the line, up the street, and out of sight. Gone, I think, forever.

Amanda chimes in as if this is some kind of personal insult to her, "Why him? Why not me?"

"Will someone shut that woman up?" says Ely.

His harsh response is too much for me to take. "Don't talk to her like that. She lost her children and when she came to you for help, you snubbed her."

"And you know what she was prepared to do to get those brats back. You were in the next room, you heard. How can you, of all people, have sympathy for someone like that?"

"Because she was thinking of her kids, not

herself. And who the hell you are to judge? What have you and your little ghost posse done besides destroy a town and everyone in it? Look at these people. They've been wrung dry, with nothing left and nowhere to go. If that was your plan, you've succeeded. So whatever's next, just do it and be done."

Silence on all sides except for Amanda, who weeps as if she's in mourning, not just for her family but for the whole town. Any anger or resentment I had for her has vanished, and I put a comforting arm around her.

"Maybe I can help," a woman says.

Everybody turns around to see Missy holding one of the jars I saw in her basement. She circles Amanda and pours the contents onto the dirt. Then she breaks off two twigs from a tree and raises them to the sky. In a language I neither know nor understand, she begins to chant.

There's a crack of thunder as if Missy's prayer has been answered. I don't know if it was her invocation or Amanda's tears, but droplets of rain begin to sprinkle down. The sprinkling turns into a downpour that drenches us all. I don't know what she's trying to prove, but all it succeeds in doing is making everyone wet and angry.

"First, they burn us, then they drown us."

The crowd starts to turn against Missy until Betty and Amanda stand up for her.

"Screw with her and you screw with the Trout sisters."

Rob, too, steps up to protect his wife. Others pick sides and it looks as though a whole new battle is about to break out.

Then Betty notices something to her left and

screams, "Oh my God!"

The beating rain has formed silhouettes around dozens of young bodies, boys and girls of all ages. These are not Ely's brood.

"Erin, Bruce?"

Amanda's children answer with voices that sound both present yet other-worldly, "Hi Mommy. Hi Daddy."

"Are you all right?"

"You're not mad at us, are you?"

"Mad? No, why would we be mad?"

Amanda reaches out to her children, but her arms slip through the ephemeral forms.

"Why can't I...I want to hold you so much."

"Soon, Mom. You have to make things right."

"What do you mean?"

"Make it right for *them*, Mommy," says Bruce.

"We will, I promise," Amanda says. "And then you'll come back to us, won't you?"

The parents huddle around the silhouettes of their children—attempting to embrace them, though it's impossible. Missy has at least given them a glimmer of hope.

"You did good, Missy."

She smiles, but I can see her struggling as the strength in her arms begins to wane and the tree limbs sag. With that, the rain's intensity decreases, and the children fade.

"Not yet, Missy, not yet, please..." Amanda cries.

"Make it right, make it right..." the children plead.

Missy's arms finally drop to her sides. The

rain ceases altogether and the children vanish. All that's left are their voices which echo into nothingness. The frustrated parents turn on Missy once again.

"Bring them back! Bring them back!"

This time, it's me who stands up for her, "Leave her alone, all of you. Your children are okay. They're safe. She just proved it. Now, do your part."

"What part are we responsible for?"

I point to the phantoms that remain lined up across the street. "Don't you get it? You're not getting your children back until we've helped them. So stop your bitching, think of someone else, and then maybe something will change." I don't know why I said "we." It's as if this town and its troubles have become mine. But I must have gotten through to them for the simple fact that they haven't strung me up from the nearest street lamp.

With a sorrowful look in her eye, Amanda turns to her husband, "Rob, there's something I need to tell you." She looks at her husband as if seeing him for the first time.

"Honey, let's get the kids back first. Then there'll be time for talk."

The two hug and seem at peace for the moment. It makes me feel a little ashamed for having stood in judgment of them. Maybe a little envious too.

"Thank you, Amanda, for being so forth coming," says Ely. "Who's next?"

No one raises a hand or even dares to twitch.

"Missy, can I see that scrying mirror of yours?"

Missy digs out the crazy-looking mirror and

hands it to Ely.

He examines it. "Fascinating things, mirrors. Generally meant to reflect a person's external features–eyes, lipstick, and makeup. But not this one. This one is used to reveal someone's inner nature." He looks over the assembled crowd as if he's about to select someone for an experiment. "Deputy, why don't you give it a try?"

"Don't know if you've noticed, numb-nuts, but I can't see."

"Why are you doing this, Ely?" asks Clarke.

"Remember what I said earlier? 'Before this night is over each one of you will face your darkest fears.' You want your children back. To do that, you'll have to unearth some long-buried truths. And the best place to start is with yourself." With that, he holds the mirror out for Art.

The deputy senses it and reluctantly places the mirror in front of his face. After a moment, his face contorts, startled by the vision he "sees" before him. From somewhere deep inside, a moan escapes that runs from surprise, to horror, to surrender. I have no idea what he saw, but whatever it is, it's profound.

"Hubble," he whimpers, "did you ever do stuff you knew was wrong?"

"What kind of stuff, Art?"

"Bad things. Things you sometimes do without thinking how it affects anybody else?"

With that said, Art pulls his weapon.

"Art, put the gun down," warns the constable.

"It's my fault."

"No, it's not."

"Yes it is. I see that now."

"Put the gun down," says his boss firmly.

Art doesn't obey. Instead, he aims the gun at his own head. "A man can't change his nature, and he can't change the past."

"Art, listen to me. You're not the only one who's made a mistake."

The look on the deputy's face has become as opaque and unfathomable as the scrying mirror. I don't know if he's listening anymore, but Clarke keeps talking, "Art, I gave up on Missy when I should've stuck by her. But here's the thing—if we decided to end it every time we made a mistake..."

Amanda crosses to Art. "Arthur, we all have our faults. We're all haunted by ghosts. The answer is not in ending it, the answer is trying to fix it."

Hubble steps over and gently asks for the gun. After a long, agonizing moment, Art relaxes and gives up the weapon.

Hubble turns to Ely, "Happy now?"

"Happy-er. Mister Malefant, how about you?" He offers the mirror to me! Haven't I done enough for this town already? Besides, I've got nothing to do with their problems. There is no way I'm letting this guy into my head. "No thanks, I'm good."

Missy steps up, "Ely, there will be time for that later. Alex is right. We need to help them get their answers," she says, pointing to the ghost children.

"We already know who's responsible for that fire," snaps the mayor, "The Dunbar Gang."

"I'm not so sure. The version I heard," says the constable, "was that it was a bunch from Fergus who came to steal back the trophy after they lost it that year."

189

"Mayor," says Missy, "your wife, Mary, said the Dunbar Gang came to your house and asked you to find their killers. So how could they be responsible?"

"I don't care what anyone says," shouts the mayor. "It was the Dunbar Gang—Brad, Andy, and Doreen."

"And there was something about a fourth member, wasn't there?" says Big Nathan with an accusatory tone.

CHAPTER 19

"Nathan, you don't know nothin' about nothin'."

Nathan shakes his thick head as if he knows something that can no longer be denied.

"C'mon, Percy. You had a crush on Doreen way back. I remember—followed her around like a little puppy dog."

Percy Novak takes a threatening step toward Nathan. "Liar! How could you even say something like that with my wife standing right here? Don't you have any respect?"

Mary exclaims, "Percy!"

It's not out of surprise but more a request to come clean.

"You can bluster all you want," Nathan continues, "but I know better."

The mayor's face grows as red as one of those prize-winning beets. "No matter what you think you know..."

The sound of a car engine revving its motor catches us all by surprise. We look down the street to see Zack, Sally, and Doug sitting in Mayor Novak's old red truck.

"Hey Stubby," shouts Zack, "we got er' goin' for you."

"Get out of my truck! That belonged to my father," shouts Percy.

Mary Novak lifts her hand to her mouth. "That old thing hasn't worked in years."

Sally sticks her head out of the rear passenger window and shouts, "Hey Mary, wanna come for a ride?"

The mayor's wife walks toward the truck, compelled to join the three spirits.

"Mary, where are you going? Come back here!"

She ignores her husband's pleas and continues up the street. The passenger door opens, and she climbs in.

"Mary, what are you doing?" screams the mayor.

Zack shouts back, "Find us our killer, Stubby, or say goodbye to wifey."

"Hubble, stop them," orders the mayor. "They're kidnapping my wife!"

"Looks to me like she went willingly."

"Shoot the tires. Shoot the ghosts too if ya have to."

The truck revs up again, makes a U-turn, and peels down the street with Mary Novak in the back seat. Percy and some others give chase, but Ely and the ghost children form a line across the road preventing anyone from crossing it. Nobody wants a confrontation. We all know what these creatures are capable of. Hubble turns back to Percy.

"They seem to know you and Mary pretty well."

"We all went to school together back then. But I wasn't in the gang, okay?"

"You just wanted to be," adds Big Nathan.

Mayor Novak doesn't answer, but it's obvious the remark has some truth to it.

"What happened that night, Percy?" asks Clarke.

"Nothing. It wasn't my fault," he answers like a petulant child. The mayor has been putting on quite a show up until now, but at this point, nobody's buying it. Novak starts to sweat. I think he knows he's at a crossroads and that whatever he's been hiding all these years will have to come out.

His swaggering persona deflates like a punctured balloon, and in the tiniest voice, he says, "I was only fourteen. They made me do it."

"It's okay, Percy," prods Missy. "Anything you can tell us..."

He sucks in a breath and then, in a slow staccato fashion, begins laying out the facts, careful not to incriminate himself.

"It was 1964. Fergus had won the festival trophy for as many years as people could remember. No matter what we challenged them at, they won. We all knew they cheated, we just didn't know how. Anyway, we were due. We were owed. This year, things would be different. I came up with a plan. I made a replica of the trophy out of clay and wrapped it in tinfoil–a pretty good copy if I do say so myself—and then I switched the real one for the fake before the prize was awarded. So even if those bastards from Fergus won again, they'd be taking home the bogus trophy, and the real one would stay in Elora where it belonged. Everybody knows Elora is the number one town in Wellington County. The best pies, the largest pumpkins..."

"You're not campaigning for office, Percy. Try to stay on point," says Hubble.

Percy snorts. "Not much more to tell. When I got to the school, the fire had already started. The flames were way too big for me to handle. I was only fourteen, like I said, so I drove back to town to get help. By the time the fire brigade showed up, the flames had done their worst."

The constable and I look at each other. Then he says, "So Percy, are you claiming a bunch from Fergus set the fire because they lost the contest, or because they won the contest and they found out the trophy was a fake?"

Percy shrugs.

"That shrug doesn't do much to plug the big gaping hole in your story," says Hubble.

I have to confess I'm becoming more confused as the story spools out. One version is that the kids from Fergus set the fire, and another suggests the Dunbar Gang are the victims of their own misfortune, yet they're the ones urging us to find their killer. In any case, I can't believe that whole disaster centered around some lousy trophy.

"Where is it now?" asks the constable.

"What?"

"The trophy. Where is it?"

"Perished in the fire, I guess. Why would that even matter?" snorts the mayor.

"So it might still be somewhere on the school grounds?" asks Missy.

Constable Clarke takes a few steps in the direction of the school, but Big Nathan shouts, "It ain't there if that's where you're goin'. Like Percy said, the old school burnt down. That one down the road is the rebuilt one."

"So where would the original one've stood, Nathan?" I ask.

"Out there on the Bernacky farm. Where the pumpkin patch is."

The significance of this hits Missy like a brick in the head. "Do you mean to say that our award-winning pumpkins come from the ashes of the children who died in that fire fifty years ago?

Hubble, we need to find that trophy."

"Why?" asks Big Nathan.

"Because that's what started this whole thing. I have a feeling that when we find it, the rest of the puzzle will fall into place."

"I vote with Missy," I add.

"You got no vote," says Big Nathan. "You're not one of us, you're just some travelling insurance salesman."

"He's as much a part of this as anyone," Missy answers in my defense. "He was here when this began, and he's stuck here till it ends. Besides, we're in no position to turn down anybody's help—unless you have this figured out by yourself, Nathan."

Nathan shrugs his burly shoulders and backs off. "No skin off my ass."

I'm not sure why, but Nathan acts like a man with something to hide. Meanwhile, the constable walks determinedly up to the ghost children. Ely signals them to let him through. Missy, myself, the mayor, and the rest of the group follow. We're going out there to look for a hunk of metal, but it feels more like we're going to dig up a grave.

CHAPTER 20

"They rebuilt the school in a different location?" I ask Missy.

"A lot of the town went that way. The hotel you're staying at was originally a gristmill. The park where the festival was held used to be a gas station. The sculpture, 'The Tall Guy' was actually erected up the street before it was moved to the park."

"Elora seems to shift with the times."

"Like the truth."

Minutes later, we're at the side of the road looking at a pumpkin patch sprawled out over two or three acres of land. Constable Clarke points to some tire tracks leading into the mucky field. Percy's truck is sitting out there about a hundred yards ahead of us with its floodlights gleaming in the fog.

"Mary?" shouts the mayor.

The only answer he gets is the distant squawking of crows, which throws a chill into all of us, especially Art.

"You sure we're doing the right thing?" asks Betty, in an attempt to convince herself more than anyone.

"What if it's a big, fat trap?" asks Big Nathan.

Missy takes the first step onto the field and the rest of us follow.

"No way I'm going out there," Art says.

"That's okay, Art, you stay right where you are," says Missy.

"No way I'm stayin' by myself either," he

replies.

Art takes a few tentative steps, and Betty jogs back to help him. As we draw closer to the truck, the constable draws his gun. When we get about twenty feet from the vehicle, he signals us to stay where we are while he creeps up on the cab to peek through the rear window.

"Mary?" Mayor Novak can't hold himself back and charges up. When he gets to the truck, he pushes the constable out of the way. "Mary, Honey, are you all right?"

"I guess so," she answers.

We all converge on the truck to find Mary sitting in the back seat alone looking like she's just woken from a dream. Everyone is relieved to find her safe. Then Big Nathan points to something up ahead in the floodlights. "What the hell?"

We follow his gaze to a spot where half a dozen crows stand in silence. Another group from overhead joins its brethren, and together, they form a semicircle.

"Is this your murder of crows?" asks Amanda. "Are we all going to die now?"

"No, this is something different," says Big Nathan. "I've never seen one myself, but I heard about it. If I'm right, this is what's known as 'a *parliament* of crows.'"

"A what?" asks Clarke.

"There are stories about crows, how intelligent they are, how they even hold court and stand in judgment of each other. The way I heard it is one or more of these critters does something to piss off the others. They hold a court or a parliament. The accused states its case, and the flock renders its judgment. If it's thumbs up, all is forgiven and they go their own way. If it's thumbs down, the flock rips the accused into pieces. Savage, quick, and final."

"Oh God," Art whimpers. "I don't wanna die." He drops to his knees and covers his face, terrified that his fate rests in the "hands" of these winged assassins. I don't blame him. The poor guy has already had a taste of their wrath and knows what's in store. The rest of us look for rocks and sticks, anything we can use to protect ourselves. The constable aims his gun at the birds. But the crows don't attack. They just sit and wait.

Missy offers a different theory. "I don't think they want a fight. I think they're trying to tell us something."

"So now you're a crow-whisperer?" asks Betty, her memory fresh from the incident with the wolves. Her sister's single-worded admonishment, "Betty," is enough to shut her up. Missy takes a few brave steps toward the birds.

"Are you sure?" cautions Officer Clarke.

I would expect him to be protective of his girlfriend, but he also knows that when Missy makes up her mind to do something, she generally follows through. The constable crosses over to flank her. Amanda, Rob, Percy, and I follow closely for moral support, leaving Art, Mary, and Big Nathan by the truck. The crows wait. When Missy reaches the semi-circle, she signals us to stop and remain silent while she assesses the situation. Then she kneels down and starts clawing the dirt with her hands. The crows watch. The rest of us follow suit. After a few minutes, she finds something. "Hubble?"

The two of them use their fingers to etch

around the circumference of an object they've unearthed. The thing looks to be about two-and-a-half feet long by a foot wide. They lift it from its shallow grave. Hubble wipes away the muck with his sleeve to reveal the battered and burnt trophy.

"Sonofabitch," says the mayor.

"Is this the real one or the fake, Percy?"

Mayor Novak runs his fingers along the metal. "It's the real McCoy."

"Now what?" asks Amanda.

"I'm not sure," Missy says. "I only know that we were meant to find it. This was your idea, wasn't it, Alexander?"

I nod. "I was hoping it would give us some kind of clue."

"Ow!" Art is standing by the truck cradling his hand. He's been bitten by one of those nasty critters. We turn around just in time to see another crow swoop down on Betty. She screams and swats at it, but the bird evades her. The attack seems to provoke the birds in front of us who flex their wings and caw belligerently.

"Truce is over, back to the truck," shouts the constable.

He scoops the rusty souvenir up in his arms and we all race back. Luckily, we make it without being harmed. Maybe this was just a warning.

Constable Clarke, Missy, and Art climb into the cab while I join the others in the cargo bay. But when the constable turns the key, the motor fails. This does not sit well with the crows that start to dive-bomb us as we sit there, open targets.

"Pointy-beaked assassins!" shouts Betty as she whips a clod of earth at one of them.

"Stop it. You're gonna make it worse,"

shouts Big Nathan.

"What do you suggest, we sit here and let 'em peck our eyes out like they did to Arthur?" She hurls another dirt clod at her tormentors. Unfortunately, she's a lousy aim and it only infuriates the flock. The women cover their heads with their arms while the men whip off their shirts and try to beat the birds away. But we're no match for a murder of crows bent on taking us out. Thankfully, the motor turns over and the truck tears out of the pumpkin patch, careening over grooves and gullies as we flip-flop like a school of landed fish.

"Thanks for bringing us out here, Alex," shouts the mayor. "Great idea."

When we reach the road, the birds suddenly break off their attack. It's almost as if they were herding us off their property. Clarke steers the truck back toward town. I have no idea what we've accomplished until we approach the outskirts to find something we haven't seen in hours, maybe days. Light. Ever since this freakish misadventure began, it's been black as night, but in the distance we can see what looks like the glow of dawn illuminating the town. Have we finally come to the end of this nightmare? If no one else is going to congratulate me for bringing us to this end, I will.

CHAPTER 21

When we turn onto Metcalfe Street, the pickup screeches to a halt. What we see is not daylight exactly, but a town drenched in shades of sepia. The entire scene looks like an old-time moving picture. Other aspects of the town have changed too. The buildings look new but from a previous era. People stroll lazily along the pitted roads. Children play hopscotch, hula-hoop, and shoot alleys. A banner stretching across the street reads, "ELORA HARVEST FESTIVAL, OCTOBER 31, 1964." We climb out of the pickup and walk toward this vision, or should I say, *into* this vision, amongst townsfolk who seem oblivious to us.

"Are we...is this...?" whispers Betty.

"Heaven? I don't think so," says Mary.

"Maybe we're in the multiplex Art was talking about," suggests Angie. Some of the others look at her questioningly, so she goes on to explain. "It's like going into one of those theatre complexes and a bunch of movies are playing at the same time. We walked into *Elora in the Sixties*."

Angie has mixed up her terms, substituting multiplex for multiverse, but her analogy isn't that far off.

Missy gives me a pat. "You were right, Alex, the trophy was the key. Just not the way you thought."

A single pump gas station stands in the spot where the park was, or is, or will be. Just north of that is a patchwork field where the festival of '64 is currently being held. Paper banners erected around the perimeter of the field name the four districts: "ELORA," "EAST FERGUS," "WEST FERGUS," and "BRIDGEWATER." Beneath the banners are tables of homemade goods from the areas they represent. There's also a show tent for horses, a display of the latest farm equipment from the day, and a hay maze where kids dressed in Halloween costumes run amok.

"Okay. Now what?" asks Big Nathan.

Officer Clarke carries the crumpled old trophy to the podium and waits to see what happens next. For the moment, nothing does so we watch the festival like a bunch of invisible interlopers. In one corner of the field there's a tug-of-war between a bunch of preteens. In another corner, giant pumpkins are lined up to be weighed. The food tables are being inspected by four judges who sample and record their scores on clipboards.Everybody seems to be having a fine time until, in the midst of all the fun and frivolity, the sound of a coarse reprimand rings out.

"Percy! Percy Novak!"

A matronly harridan to whom the voice belongs comes into view, followed by her rail-thin husband. They elbow their way through the crowd toward a young boy perhaps thirteen or fourteen years old. He's a sullen, chubby kid who sits on the sidelines while other kids play horseshoes. Upon hearing his name, he reluctantly shuffles over to his parents. Young Percy's mother grabs him by the collar and gives him a shake, "What did I tell you about wandering away? You stay close where I c'n see ya."

"Okay, but after, I'm goin' to the dance."

"You ain't goin' nowhere," says his father.

"You're helpin' your ma with her pies."

"Lord knows I get no help from you," replies the Missus to her Mister.

"But you promised!" wails Young Percy.

"Mind your manners, Boy, and no back-talk," scolds his father. The words are meant more to appease his wife. Seems as though Percy's old man has no backbone. Mayor Novak cringes at the treatment his younger self endures at the hands of his parents, and mutters, "Jesus, once wasn't enough?"

A few yards away, three teenagers whisper conspiratorially and then disperse as if on a secret mission.

"That's them there," says the mayor. "Brad Dunbar, Andy Greco, and Doreen Pierce. The Dunbar Gang."

Doreen approaches one of the merchants with a mischievous gleam in her eye. The merchant is Big Nathan—that is, a younger, smaller version of himself. "Hey there, Nate, how many pieces could I get out of a pie this size, ya think?"

Young Nathan turns his attention to Doreen. It's clear he has a thing for the pretty, young girl. "Well, lemme see here, Sweetie, about eight I guess."

"And this one?"

While Doreen distracts Young Nathan, Andy steals a pie from the table and hands it to Brad who strolls off in the opposite direction before anyone is the wiser. Doreen thanks Young Nathan for his help and promises to come back later with her mother to buy the pie.

"The little bitch!" mutters Big Nathan as he realizes he was scammed.

An official steps up to the podium and calls for the crowd's attention. He welcomes everyone to the annual event, introduces the judges, and announces the three contests that will determine the overall winner of the festival: the tug-of-war, the largest pumpkin, and the tastiest pie. Then he raises the trophy that the constable placed on the stand. Somehow, it has morphed into its original, brilliant form. As the crowd shouts enthusiastically, the official directs everyone's attention to the tug-of-war. The preteens are shoo'd away to allow the adults to take up the rope for the real competition. The crowd hustles over to cheer on their champions. Young Percy watches the official place the trophy back on its stand and leave it there. This being a small town, I suppose nobody has any worries about leaving the trophy unattended. They should.

Over at the food tasting area, we see the judges conferring before they make their selection and narrow down the choices. The pies chosen are all brought to a table next to the podium.

Missy tries to tell us about something she noticed back at the original staging area, but we're all too caught up watching Young Percy race over to his father's truck. He reaches into the cargo bay and pulls out a blanket with something heavy wrapped inside. He looks around to make sure no one is watching, then hustles back to the podium to unwrap the object—a crude copy of the trophy.

"Percy, I thought you said Fergus won and you drove over that night and stole the trophy back," Betty says.

The mayor doesn't answer—just looks at the ground, ashamed. When no one is looking, Young Percy places the fake trophy on the stand, wraps the real one in the blanket, and runs it back to his father's truck.

After this sequence, the entire scene fades like a curtain going down on a play. The sepia light dissolves, and we're cloaked once again in ink-black night.

"You lied," says Betty to Percy. "You made the switch before the trophy was even awarded. Why?"

"I told you. Every year it was the same. Fergus would cheat us and then they'd beat us. It wasn't fair. If nobody else was gonna do anything about it, I was."

I don't get it. "What does stealing the trophy have to do with anything?"

The mayor doesn't reply, but as if the cosmos itself is answering, the light dawns once again, and we find ourselves at the original school in the pumpkin field. It's a long, single-storey building, sectioned off into classrooms with a gym at one end. Popular songs of the 60s are playing inside. This is the school's Halloween dance, the scene where all those children died tragically. I don't know if I have the stomach to witness that.

The roar of a big engine signals a vehicle racing down the bumpy road—Percy's father's red pickup. It stops in a cloud of dust. Young Percy jumps out of the cab and jogs over to a window. The stocky kid is a bundle of nerves. He peeks inside, and when he finds who he's looking for, he raps on the window. Young Percy steps back and paces until three teens shuffle out of the gym–Brad, Andy, and Doreen. As soon as they appear, Andy lights a cigarette and passes it around.

"I did it!" brags Young Percy. "I got it, man,

just like I told ya!"

Brad smirks with an easy cool, "Yeah, let's see."

Young Percy leads them back to his father's truck, pulls out the blanket we saw earlier, and unwraps the original trophy he stole.

"Sonofabitch, he really did it," says Andy.

"'Course I did, just like I told ya. So now I'm in, aren't I?"

Young Percy glances at Doreen, hoping for a positive response. It looks like someone has a heavy crush. Doreen doesn't give Young Percy the reaction he expected. Instead, she defers to Brad who stands there with a sly grin.

"Almost. There's just one more thing for the initiation: you gotta kiss Andy's naked ass."

The eager smile on Young Percy's face quickly fades. "You're jokin'! You said it was just about the trophy."

Brad shrugs as if to say it's out of his hands. Andy unzips his pants and pulls down his jeans, offering his butt cheeks to Young Percy. The boy looks to Doreen with a silent plea for intervention, but she reacts with the same casual shrug as Brad. Poor kid. If he does as he's told, he'll be humiliated in front of the girl he most wants to impress. If he doesn't, he won't get into the gang, and he'll lose any respect he might have gained by pulling off this stunt.

"Come on, man, it's cold out here," says Andy who wiggles his ass to the amusement of his friends.

Young Percy looks undecided, and he hesitates. The elderly Percy standing beside me bites his lip to keep from screaming out in anger. It looks like Young Percy is going to go through with it until, from the corner of my eye, I notice a girl watching through the partially open gym door. It's Mary, the mayor's wife, as a young teen. Knowing that she's watching, Young Percy realizes there's no way he can complete the act. Brad gestures for Andy to zip up his pants, takes a drag from the cigarette, and sighs, "Too bad, Man. You were so close." The bully flicks his cigarette at Young Percy.

Andy grabs the trophy from him. "Thanks, man. I'll take that."

Young Mary shrinks back behind the gym door as the three members of the Dunbar Gang swagger back into the school, leaving Young Percy feeling humiliated and ashamed. The kid kicks the ground and swears to himself. After they leave, he breaks down in tears.

"You had no intention of righting a wrong or standing up for the town, didja, Percy?" asks the constable. "All you wanted was to get into the gang."

Betty and the others avoid direct eye contact with the mayor. I guess we've all been in similar situations and felt the sting of rejection. Meanwhile, the scenario continues to play out. Young Percy wipes his face and notices the cigarette butt burning on the ground. A nasty, vengeful look comes into his eyes.

"What're you up to, Percy?" asks the constable.

Young Percy gathers some stray papers and wood chips and shoves them under the gym door. He picks up the cigarette butt and blows on the flame. Then the kid does exactly what we're afraid he's going to do and lights the kindling with the glowing cigarette. Surely, he's not going to punish all the children for the crimes of three punks?

We look at the elderly mayor for some kind of explanation, but he refuses to acknowledge us. The flames ignite, but the fire threatens to sputter out. Young Percy looks around for more things to feed it–gum wrappers, garbage, and such—and pretty soon, the blaze grows. When it becomes impressive enough, he runs into the gym. Betty and Amanda rush over to douse the fire, but they have no effect on this alternate plane. Even so, Constable Clarke, Missy, and I run to the closest window to warn those inside, but are frustrated by the same result. The elder Percy remains rooted to the spot, all too aware of what's about to happen next.

Inside the gym, Brad, Doreen, and Andy are bragging to a group of kids, showing off the trophy as if it was theirs. The door swings open and Young Percy appears. Everyone turns to stare and laugh. It looks as if the Dunbar Gang told everyone what happened outside, and Young Percy has become the butt of the joke–no pun intended.

The elder Percy finally speaks up in his defense, "I was going to warn them that there was a fire—that they should get out. I didn't mean for anyone to get hurt."

I snort. "You set the fire so you could rush in there and play hero?"

Percy nods. "But no one would listen. They were too busy laughing at me."

The kids in the gym turn and giggle at Young Percy–everyone, except Young Mary. Taunts and jeers continue to antagonize until Young Percy leaves the gym, followed by Young Mary.

208

The two burst through the school doors into the yard to find acrid plumes of smoke billowing everywhere. Fire has caught onto the exterior and travels along the wood struts, engulfing the entire building like a greedy beast. Young Percy makes a sorry attempt at kicking the door frame to try to snuff out the fire, but there's nothing he can do. He turns and shouts, "Get out of there, Mary. Run!"

Young Mary won't leave. She's afraid to desert her classmates. Out of options, Young Percy runs back to his father's truck, climbs in, and drives out of the parking lot. Mary hurries over to the window and bangs on it to get everyone's attention, but the music is too loud for anyone to hear her. She goes back to stamp out the ever-growing flames, but there's no way. The fire is the length of the schoolhouse roof now, eating its way through the building.

The sepia tones dim as the fire consumes the entire structure. Mercifully, we're spared the horror of standing by as the children perish. Instead, we're transported from tragedy to merriment when we find ourselves back at the festival with the residents gathered around the podium. Young Percy jumps out of his truck and races over just as the contest winners are being announced. When he asks for help, he's drowned out by the enthusiastic shouting. Frustrated, Young Percy notices Young Titus and Young Nathan watching the ceremonies from a discreet distance and hurries over. "Titus, Titus!" he begs.

"Hush, Boy. The judges're makin' their decision. I have a feelin' Elora's gonna take the prize this year."

"I got the same feelin'," says Young Nathan.

A conspiratorial smile passes between the two.

"But the school..." cries Young Percy.

"Shut it," command both men.

The judges finish conferring and make their decision. One of them raises a pie tin and pulls the label off the bottom to read the name that has been printed on it.

"This year's winner of the best pie in Wellington County is...Angie Sullivan."

When he announces the winners, all of the residents of Elora cheer. Young Titus and Young Nathan smile at each other.

"Titus and Nathan seemed pretty certain about the win," I wonder aloud.

"Come over here," Missy says. She leads the group back to the former staging area and points at a few labels that lay in the dirt. "That's what I was trying to tell you before. Somebody tore off the originals and replaced them with others before the selection advanced to the finals."

All eyes turn to Big Nathan.

"It was only fair. We were due," he says.

Meanwhile, a judge reaches for the trophy sitting on the podium and notices how awkward it feels in his hands. Upon realizing the trophy is a fake, the crowd, who has been waiting years for this victory, becomes enraged. Young Percy lets out an involuntary laugh.

"You have something to do with that, Boy?" asks Titus.

"No, I swear. Anyway, you have to listen. There's a fire at the school!"

"Sure there is," Young Titus shakes his head in disbelief. "Percy Novak, I've known you a long time and I know when you're lyin'. Now you answer my question. Did you have anything to do with that fake trophy? And are you crying wolf to distract us from the truth?"

Young Percy clams up, afraid to say another word. Some of the citizens who have overheard the conversation gang up on the boy, demanding to know where the real trophy is.

The elder Percy sighs and explains with bitter remorse, "By the time people believed me it was too late."

The sepia-toned scene fades, and our sorry group is left in the empty park under this insufferable darkness.

Mary takes her husband's arm protectively. "I tried to warn everyone at the gym, but they wouldn't listen. No one ever listened to me. I wasn't one of the cool kids. When they finally did, it was too late. The roof started to collapse. Everyone rushed to the door at the same time. Kids were trampled. Some got out. Some didn't."

"I…I'm sorry," says Mayor Percy in the tiniest, most sorrowful voice I've ever heard.

CHAPTER 22

Upon hearing how the children actually died fifty years ago, the residents of Elora direct their anger toward the mayor. But before anyone can lay a hand on him, Constable Clarke steps up.

"It wasn't just Percy. Everyone in this town is to blame. You could have listened to the boy, but you were more interested in some stupid trophy."

"It was ours for the winning!" howls Big Nathan. There's a hollowness in his words.

Ely Shrill appears at the edge of the park encircled by his young spirits. "Guilt ran rampant in the days after," he says. "It drenched the whole town in shame. No one ever moved past this tragedy."

"No one except Titus," Missy says.

"Why him?" asks Big Nathan.

Looking back, I remember Titus having that heart-to-heart with Ely on his porch. When I dropped in on him afterward, I heard music and saw those dancing shadows. Both he and Big Nathan switched the labels to ensure the win, but Titus was the only one who owned up to his part in the tragedy.

And that's what he was doing when he approached the phantoms on the street—handing them some of the labels he stole—so that when his wife and daughter appeared, they were able to lead him to a place none of the others could go.

In the framework of everything I've witnessed, it makes sense. But not everyone is convinced.

"This is a load of bull, all of it," says Betty.

"Are you trying to say we're not real, Mister Shrill? That I'm a ghost or something?"

"You're real, Betty, and so are they," he says, pointing to the spirits. "Think of all of us as existing at the same time on different levels, in parallel lines. Generally, these lines don't cross, but it could be that Elora is at the nexus of something, a terminal of sorts where time has the ability to intersect allowing realities to collide."

I keep going back to Titus's remark, "it's in the dirt."

"It never happened before. Why now?" asks Nathan.

"It's Halloween for one," says Angie. "A time where everybody dresses up as someone they'd rather be. That's kind of an alternate reality, isn't it?"

"We've had Halloweens in the past and nothing like this has ever happened," remarks Amanda. "So what's different about this Halloween?"

Everybody looks around. Slowly, all heads turn to...

"It's not me," is all I can say.

I've never been here before nor do I have a single relative or friend living here. There is no way I can be blamed for a tragedy that happened fifty years ago in a town I never visited.

"You have to admit, Alexander," says Missy, "when you arrived, that's when things started going wonky."

I certainly have no superpowers to bend time. I'm just an insurance salesman. But what if I *am* here for a reason? "I'm not saying I'm responsible, but what if I'm here as a witness so that if Elora ever gets tangled up in a parallel universe or fades into the mist like Brigadoon, I'll be left to tell the story?"

"Something to consider, Alexander." Says Missy.

Mayor Novak shuffles over to Constable Clarke and in a tone tinged with genuine remorse, says, "Thank you, Hubble. For what it's worth nobody ever stood up for me before."

"I feel bad that you got picked on as a kid, Percy, but you set a fire and a lot of people died."

"I know, I know."

Maybe after time and reflection, Percy and the others will find the same release as Titus did. But something else bothers me. If the quest for those responsible for the fire is over, if the culprit has been found and the truth revealed, what are those ghost children still doing here? That's when I notice Missy observing the families who have been reunited, and I think, *Why am I so stupid?* Over by the bridge, I notice one child standing by herself, maybe six or seven years old. And I get it. *She* is the missing piece to the puzzle. "So Missy, you asked me earlier about the child who led me to you in the forest."

"Yes."

"I think I know why I'm here. Not to be witness to some crazy time warp or to record a fairy tale for posterity. The one I've been chasing ever since I arrived is your daughter, Chloe."

I point to the child.

CHAPTER 23

"Are you sure, Alexander?"

"Yes, and this was why I was brought here, Missy—to bring you and her together. To bring you peace of mind."

She nods. "You still don't understand, do you?"

"Me? I don't think you understand..."

"Why did all this happen now, do you think?"

"I dunno. Maybe like Angie said, because Halloween is the one night where we can pretend to be the kind of people we'd like to be? To live in an alternate reality?"

"Or have we been living in an alternate reality until now? You had a daughter too, remember?"

I nod.

"When did she die?"

"Four years ago."

"When did she die, exactly, Alexander?" she repeats.

A coincidence, I tell myself as sweat starts to trickle down my back. "So my daughter died on Halloween. What does that prove? Is this some kind of game, some kind of malicious trick you're playing? After all I've..."

The girl on the bridge opens the trunk of my car and takes out one of the dolls. She examines it and tosses it over the bridge, into the river.

"What are you doing? Stop that! You have no right!" I scream.

I make a run for the bridge but a flock of

crows flies at me, blocking me from getting any further. "What the hell is this? One of those trial things, one of those parliament of crows?"

Missy offers me that damn scrying mirror again. I take it to appease her, but there's no way I'm looking into it.

"So, Alex, that night you lost your daughter?" Missy prods.

"Look, everything that's been going on in your little town, it's not my problem. I did my best. But you have to finish it yourself."

"Alex, just indulge me," purrs Missy.

My personal life is none of her goddamn business. I knew I shouldn't have gotten so involved. I need to get out of here, but even if I get past her and the others, I'll never outrun those damn crows. The only thing I can do is to be patient until I can find a way out. "All right. It was Halloween. We were at the Dwyer's home."

"The Dwyers?" asks Missy.

"My boss at Hale Insurance. Fergus Dwyer and his wife. They host these corporate get-togethers every year for their employees."

"And the weather that evening?" asks Amanda.

"Indian summer, one of the hottest on record. I remember because the kids were out on the streets before it got dark. No jackets. Darlene and I had to do some shopping—groceries and candies for the trick-or-treaters. The three of us ran the errands before we swung by the party."

"Lifesavers," says Betty.

"Laura's favorite. She loved all the different colors. Anyway, we spent the required time at the Dwyers' and on the way home is when it happened."

"The accident, you mean?" asks Clarke.

"It was dark by then. And foggy. I remember we passed some punks standing at the side of the road, tossing eggs at cars. One of them hit my windshield. I tried to wipe the smear off with my windshield wipers but it just made it worse and blocked my vision. There were children everywhere. I didn't want to hurt them. So I swerved and the car went off the road, into a tree."

"A big old oak tree?" asks Ely.

"I wasn't really aware of what kind of tree. Maybe."

"That's how your daughter died?" says Missy.

"Yes. How many times do I have to live through that nightmare?"

"It was brave of you to try to avoid those children," says Amanda softly.

"That's the official story?" asks Clarke.

"That's *the* story, friend," I snap back.

"This wasn't the first party you attended at the Dwyers, was it?"

"Fergus's parties were mandatory: Christmas, Easter, summer picnics. He liked to promote a family feeling in the company, but that wasn't the real reason. It was his way of keeping tabs on his employees."

"Why, do you think?"

"Because he was a control freak. Because he was paranoid about his job and his future."

"What do you mean?"

"You think you people invented contests,

invented trophies? When I started at Hale Insurance I worked in the actuarial department. But I wasn't satisfied sitting behind a desk. I had ambition; I wanted to rise in the company. One of the ways you do that is to create your own opportunities. I developed a procedure that would streamline the insurance payout system—make it more efficient and save us money. To rise in the company and head my own department was *my* prize. Fergus was pushing me to finish because if it became standard in the industry, he would benefit right along with me. But it was October and we were up against the last fiscal quarter. The man had a huge ego and was starting to make threats to get me to hand in my report prematurely. I wasn't going to jeopardize my future by presenting some half-baked idea or it would be my ass, not his. I told Darlene about it. That was my mistake. The night of Fergus's party, I noticed both of them missing, so I went looking. I found them in the library."

"You *heard* them in the library. What were they doing?" asks Amanda.

"Darlene was trying to persuade Fergus to ease up on me."

"Trying to persuade him, how?"

I can't speak the words.

"Do I need to say it? She offered...she offered herself in exchange for me keeping my job."

"What did you do? What did you do, Alex?"

"I returned to the party and had a drink, okay?"

I can see their eyes accusing me, condemning me.

"What was I going to do, start a fistfight? I didn't do anything wrong. *She* was the one. *She* did it."

"That's right," says Percy. "It wasn't his fault just like it wasn't mine."

That's all I need! A loser like Percy coming to my defense.

"But you were never actually in the room, were you?" Amanda says. "Anything you heard was from outside the door, so you don't know exactly what happened inside."

"They were in there together, alone, okay? It didn't take much to imagine."

"Well, that's the problem, isn't it? The difference between what you imagined and what really happened."

"It was as clear as what you and Ely were up to in the room right next to me. I heard your proposition to him and I heard him turn you down."

"This room you speak of..."

"At the Elora Inn and don't deny it."

Amanda points down the street. "Alex, the Elora Inn has been closed for years."

I look down the street to where the inn stands. Incredibly, there's a chain link fence around it. The windows are shuttered and the place is vacant. How can that be?

"You *imagined* you heard us," Amanda continues, "In the same way you imagined your wife with Fergus because that justified your feelings."

"My feelings of what?"

"Feelings of guilt and self-loathing for not having the nerve to stand up to your boss."

I am so incensed by this woman and her lies,

"*You* were in that room making deals about my future behind my back."

"I was standing up for you because you didn't have the guts to do it yourself. You were more afraid of losing your job than you were of losing me! It was easier to blame me for betraying you than admitting that."

What is she saying? What am *I* saying? What is going on here?

"Are you all right, Alexander?" asks Missy.

"No. I'm, I'm not sure."

"Take your time. It can be confusing, can't it? Elora was jealous of a town named Fergus. You were jealous of a *man* named Fergus."

The coincidence registers, but there's no time to breathe before Constable Clarke is at me. "You said you had a drink or two and then you all left the party. Sounds like by the time you got your family into the car you were pretty stewed."

"I never used the word, 'stewed.'"

"You were driving home and you saw three kids on the road," Zack says.

"Throwing eggs just like you did at Missy's," I reply angrily.

"Messing up your windshield," adds the constable.

"Right. And I swerved to avoid hitting some children."

"Which is when you hit the oak tree?"

"Yes, when I hit your precious oak tree!" As the words leave my mouth, my body spasms as if experiencing it again.

"Well, I don't buy it," says Big Nathan.

"I don't give a shit what you buy, you big tub of lard!"

I'm almost at the end of my rope with this inquisition, when Missy steps in to defend me, "We're not here to crucify this man. We're here to help. Alex, you're doing great. We're almost there." She gestures to the scrying mirror, but no way am I submitting to that.

"It doesn't matter, Missy," says Clarke. "It's all in the police report." Which he pulls from his back pocket.

"Where did you get that?" I ask, bewildered.

"I asked for this right after our children went missing. What? You didn't think I wouldn't check out the new guy?" He glances at the report. "You're right. The official report says you swerved to avoid some children on the road and hit a tree, whereupon your daughter died instantly."

The memory of that horrific moment descends upon me like a shroud. "After the initial shock, I turned to Darlene. She was hurt but conscious. Next, I turned around. Laura was lying across the back seat. Her face was turned away but her shoes, her shoes were at such an odd angle."

As torturous as that image of her shoes dangling over the car seat is, it's real. And for a moment, I feel vindicated.

"However that's not what your wife wrote in her letter," he adds.

When he pulls out this other sheet of paper I'm astounded. "What letter? Where did you get that?"

This cop, whom I trusted, the one I've come to respect, ignores my question and just ploughs on, "Your wife writes here that it was *after* the accident that she took out the eggs you bought earlier and smashed them on the windshield."

"That's absurd! Why would she write that? Why would she even do that?"

He continues, "Your daughter, Laura, was dead on impact. Darlene had lost her child, and she knew she'd lose you too because you'd be charged with drinking and driving. You went shopping earlier and put the groceries in the trunk, correct? That's where she found the eggs and smeared them over the windshield. Then you both concocted a story about being ambushed by three kids."

"That's what keeps you up at night," says Ely. "Not the work or the business reports."

"And it worked," says Betty. "After the investigation, you were released. But the truth ate at you both. The loss of your daughter, plus the lie was too much for Darlene. She left you a year later."

I can only stare blankly at these strangers and their ridiculous accusations.

"Peace of mind, Alex," coos Missy. The phrase is spoken not with sarcasm but with compassion.

"So, getting back to that night when Fergus and your wife were in the library..." continues Constable Clarke.

I am so tired. All I want is for this to be over. I open the mirror and gaze into its blackness. The man that appears to me is desperate to hold onto his lie. He's pleading with me. But through the fog of my memory, through all the layers I buried this horrendous night under, the truth drifts to the surface. "Fergus was threatening to fire me because I refused to hand in that damned report."

"It was yours for the winning, Alex," says

Big Nathan.

"You should talk, you Neanderthal! You and Titus had to switch those labels. You had to cheat to win. Not me. I refused to compromise my ethics or my integrity."

"No, you convinced yourself that your wife had sex with your boss," says Amanda. "It was easier for you to imagine that than face the fact that you didn't have the nerve to stand up to him."

"Be honest, Alex," says, the Constable, "you didn't do anything that night to stop your wife or confront your boss. What you did do was go back to the party and drink."

"No, no!" The monster in the mirror keeps telling me to deny it, but I can't listen to him anymore. "I never, ever meant to hurt my baby girl. Darlene and I were out of our minds, there was no thinking, we just acted. After that, I was a mess. I found out later that Fergus actually handed in the report–after he switched my name for his. In the end, he got what he wanted—the credit, the raise, the prize. When he couldn't face me being around the office any longer, he put me on the road."

"And you went gladly," says Missy. "To get as far away as you could. You ran from *Laura* and ended up in *Elora*. You came offering peace of mind when that's what you'd been seeking all this time."

"Hell, even a blind man can see that," says Art.

"Who is that little girl, Alexander? Who is that seven-year-old?"

I turn back to the bridge and shudder when I

realize she is no longer there. After all this, I can't bear to lose her again. The residents no longer stand in my way. I run up the street to the bridge, but when I get to my car she's gone. All I see are the dolls below, floating in the lazy current toward the falls. They gather by that outcropping, the Tooth of Time. And there, amongst the foliage, she waits. She is who I have come for, from whom I ask forgiveness. Missy was right. This is about *my* peace of mind. A sense of calm comes over me and I know what to do. I take one step onto the girder, close my eyes and leap. The water engulfs me, the cold energizes me. So refreshing after all the unbearable heat and darkness. When I break the surface, everything has changed. Sounds of children fill the air. I turn to see them on the far side of the river calling to their parents who in turn, run madly toward them. They meet on the bridge. It's a deliriously, happy moment. Then, ahead of me by the falls, the sun rises. Daylight peeks over the water's edge and spreads before me, ending the longest night of my life.

The current is calm and soothing. It guides me down the river toward a line of orange buoys. Here, the water quickens. Soon now. Behind me are the joyful sounds of reunited families. In front of me, I see her, smiling, waiting for me. "I'm coming, Laura. Daddy's coming."

www.ingramcontent.com/pod-product-compliance
Lightning Source LLC
Chambersburg PA
CBHW070106260626
47160CB00004B/1341